APRÈS-SKI

A ROMANCE NOVELLA

PHEBE POWERS

For my siblings, all of whom are better skiers than I.

CHAPTER 1
BOSTON LOGAN

"Seventeen bucks for a sandwich?" Estie stared at the sticker in disbelief.

"This *is* an airport," her younger brother pointed out, unhelpfully. "Didn't you get Mom's text last night?"

"Which text? There were rather more than several."

"The one where she told everyone in the family group chat to bring something to eat."

Estie eyed him skeptically. "Don't tell me *you* packed a meal."

Freddy shrugged. "No, but Ben made me breakfast before we left his apartment."

"At five in the morning?" She was impressed. Why didn't she have a boyfriend like that? Probably because she bolted at the first sign of commitment, typically.

Her brother smiled smugly, reading her mind. "Get your own soul-mate. Or find a job that actually pays." As Estie struggled, due to the early hour and her lack of sleep, to come up with a suitably snarky response, Freddy picked out a bag of chips, two waters, and some spearmint gum. "See you at the gate!"

Estie sighed as her brother walked away. She loved writing, she really did. But… it was hard. Self-publishing took a lot of time and effort, the actual drafting and editing of her romance novels aside. And, as her brother had so kindly pointed out, it didn't quite pay the bills. Not fully. Thank god her parents were willing and able to cover a large part of the rent on her studio. Admittedly, the little apartment was a luxury, but she needed to be alone to write. Estie had tried and failed to have both a career and roommates. Then again, maybe she just had yet to find the right person to live with. Someone who'd inspire her to add to her backlist, not stall her creative process.

"Estie!"

She whipped her head around. "Oh! Hey, Miles." Her older sister's fiancé approached, wallet in hand. "Did you and Flo forget to eat breakfast, too?"

He shook his head. "Nah, but you know how she gets if she doesn't have two cups of coffee, and we only had time for one because the taxi arrived early."

"And they couldn't wait?"

"We were lucky to get a car at all. And I wouldn't put the love of my life through an early morning ride on the Red Line." Miles laughed, ever upbeat. "Anyway, do you want me to get that for you?"

Estie shook her head rapidly. "No, no. I mean, thank you. But no. I can afford a sandwich." A brazen lie, given the sandwich in question's price, but she had her pride.

"Fair enough." Miles knew better than to argue with her, especially at an early hour. "Besides, you'll be buying all of us sandwiches, when your next book becomes a bestseller!"

Oh, Miles. He really was sweet. "Sure thing." She smiled at him blearily. Maybe she needed a coffee, too… What time even was it? Estie checked her phone. A few minutes before eight, which meant it was almost time for her to take her meds. "Actually, Miles?"

He turned back to her. "Yeah?"

"Could you get me a coffee, too? Just a bit of milk, no sugar."

Miles nodded. "Whole or skim?"

"Whole." Estie believed in living fully, and that meant not settling for white water that called itself milk. "Thanks, M!"

"No worries." He smiled again, an absolute golden retriever of a man. "I'll bring it to the gate."

Estie grabbed the sandwich, budget be damned, and made her way to the self-checkout. There, she impulse-bought some dark chocolate, too. She'd save the sandwich for the plane—her thyroid medication required an empty stomach, she reasoned—but she could munch on the chocolate bar while waiting to board.

After a brisk walk back to the gate, Estie was greeted by her entire family, minus Miles: her mother, anxiously checking the delicate wristwatch that had once belonged to Estie's grandmother; her father, belatedly engrossed in Estie's second-to-most-recent release; her sister, snoring softly in her seat; and her brother and his boyfriend, who were engaged in a very public display of affection.

Estie felt nauseated—and lonely, as per usual. She averted her eyes, a touch dramatically. "Freddy, can you stop tonguing your boyfriend's tonsils for five seconds and move your bag off that otherwise open chair?"

Her brother disentangled himself from Ben in order to glare at her. "Find your own seat."

"There's nowhere else to sit!" She gestured around the waiting area. "They're all taken."

Grumbling, Freddy moved his bag. "Fine, but you're ruining the mood."

"I'm not sure there can be much of a 'mood' given that we're in an airport and it's eight in the morning."

Ben laughed. "Estie, you write romance novels. Surely you know that airports as a setting are romantic to the point of being a cliché?"

"Only if you're running through them, Ben."

"Whatever, Estie." Freddy rolled his eyes. "Consider any and all moods ruined by you, regardless."

Estie sighed. "Blame it on my *mood* disorder." Ben shifted uncomfortably, but Freddy was unfazed. He opened his mouth to argue, but Estie held up a staying hand as she slumped into the newly vacated seat. She was too tired to hear or herself summon a smart rejoinder. Where was Miles with her coffee?

"I'm going to try and get some writing done," she announced to everyone and no one. Then she pulled her laptop from its pink, padded sleeve. Prying it apart, she found that her word processor was already open, the waiting document as menacing as Moby Dick himself in its wordless whiteness.

When it came to writing, and life, too, Estie was a pantser, through and through. But for whatever reason, in the past month, the requisite words had refused to come. She was increasingly concerned—to the extent that she'd even considered going against the grain, throwing her lack of caution to the wind, and plotting out her next novel in advance of actually writing it. Like some kind of organized, methodical, sane writer. But the only two things Estie planned meticulously were falling in love and refilling her medications—which was why, her older sister had commented, a little unkindly, she did the latter monthly and the former never.

Estie sighed and started to type, trying to wrangle her muse as well as her mood. Method wasn't the reason for her block, but a lack of inspiration. And somehow she doubted she'd find any on this family ski holiday—the first in a decade, and her recently retired parents' treat... No, for her the slopes held only terror, and not romance.

While her siblings had significant experience on mountains all across America, as well as in Canada and even (in her sister's case) the French Alps, Estie hadn't skied since she was a kid. And that had been... an experience. Not only was she undoubtedly terrible now, at twenty-five she was old enough and wise enough to be terrified.

Still, Flo had promised Estie that she'd have fun in Blue Sky, the mountain town in Montana that lent its name to the nearby ski resort, that she would find things to do if skiing didn't work out, that she wouldn't be lonely or bored—even though her whole family would be abandoning her to the mild humiliation of ski school while they shot the chutes and dared the triple black diamonds. Freddy had been raving about something called the Big Couloir, only accessible by the very exclusive (and apparently expensive) tram. Estie thought it sounded dangerous, and that anyone who went up there willingly was deranged. Her siblings included.

But, Estie had for some godforsaken reason promised her family that she would at least try. And trying meant enrolling in the afore-mentioned ski school. For a day. After that, she'd stay home at the house they were renting and, keyboard in hand, continue to plead her case with the mercurial inhabitants of her mind's Mount Parnassus.

"Flight 362 to Boseman is now boarding at Gate 18."

Estie perked up, even as her sister jerked awake.

"Are we boarding? Where's Miles? We can't forget him again—"

Chuckling, Miles appeared at his fiancée's side, balancing three cups of coffee between his triangulated fingers. "Relax, sweetheart. I'm here. But I'm afraid we all might have to chug."

Estie took her coffee gratefully even as her sister tore the lid off her own cup and muttered, "Sophomore year trained me for this…"

"Alright, team. One more trip up the Magic Carpet, then I want to see your best pizza turns all the way down. Sound good?"

A chorus of small children cheered their approval. James had lucked out today—the kids were enthusiastic and quick learners, all of them. There had only been one tearful incident, and he'd quickly remedied that with a promise of hot chocolate and a sing-along when the day was done.

James didn't usually teach kids; he preferred working with adults. But his supervisor had given him a choice between work and no work, and he couldn't afford to take more than one day off a week, what with the pittance the resort paid him. Private lessons were the only real way to make a living on the slopes, and unfortunately James had yet to build up a substantial client list. Unlike his roommate, Drew, who had a list of thirty or so clients so loyal that they'd followed him north when he left Vail for Blue Sky.

Still, James managed to make ends meet, supplementing his instructor's income with the occasional gig at one of the two bars in town. The locals might get tired of his Randy Travis covers, but the out-of-towners loved a late night rendition of "Deeper Than The Holler," and they tipped fairly well, once they'd had a few.

"Mr. James?" Kayla—who had informed him, immediately upon their introduction, that her seventh birthday was next week—tugged on the sleeve of his blue regulation ski jacket.

"Yes, Kayla?"

She gestured to her boot, which had somehow come free of its trappings. "My ski popped off."

"Do you remember how to put it back on?" James held her mittened hand so she wouldn't fall over as she balanced on one ski. There was nothing so detrimental to a student's confidence, or sense of safety, as a bad fall. Luckily, kids were pretty good at bouncing back. Better, in fact, than adults, who felt the humiliation more keenly with their grown up sensibility. It also helped that kids were shorter, which meant closer to the ground, so when they hit it, it didn't hurt so much. "Toe in first, yep, just like that. And then the heel. Stomp on it, like you're trying to kill a spider."

Kayla did as she was told, but when her boot had clicked back into place, her ski sliding a little against the packed snow, she looked up at James with eyes that were wide behind her pink-tinted goggles. "But spiders are good bugs. I don't wanna kill any spiders."

James considered this. "You're right, Kayla. I'll find a new analogy." Her nose wrinkled in clear confusion, an expression he recognized from having grown up babysitting his little cousins in Vermont; James realized he'd forgotten to adjust his vocabulary to better suit a seven year old. If she was still curious, he'd explain later. "Now, how about we join the rest of the group up on top of the slope?"

They were skiing within the confines of the designated teaching area, accessible to students and instructors only. There wasn't much to it, other than a small half-pipe where the students who were new to skis practiced the basics, and a short, not very steep slope called Lazy River. The teaching area also boasted the so-called Magic Carpet, which was really just a conveyor belt that carried skiers young and old up the miniature slope. There was another, bigger conveyor outside of the teaching area that led part of the way up a green, but James' students weren't ready for wide open spaces—or heavily trafficked areas—just yet.

Kayla inched onto the Magic Carpet, which was already whisking her peers up the hill, keeping her knees bent like they'd practiced. A few seconds later, it was James' turn. He squinted up the slope, counting helmets to make sure he hadn't forgotten a student, then shuffled onto the conveyor belt himself when he was satisfied that no child had been left behind.

At the top, the kids had spread out, hiking sideways across the ledge at the top of Lazy River. "Everybody ready?" James called out, throwing his voice so the kids could hear him above the whistling wind. They all nodded, some more dubiously than others, but generally they were a pretty fearless group. "Mike, why don't you show us how it's done? I want to see three wide turns and a nice slow stop at the bottom. No collisions."

An eight year old at the far end of the ledge saluted him. "Yes, sir!"

James saluted him right back. He'd be lying if he said he didn't enjoy the kids' respect, and how seriously they took this—unlike most people, including the majority of his family back east, who saw his seasonal gigs as well as his songwriting and singing as a couple of childhood hobbies that he'd wasted himself on, rather than budding careers to which he'd devoted the whole of his adult life. But who cared what they thought? They were estranged, after all, with the majority of them having cut him out after he'd taken his mother's side in her divorce. James sighed. Then he forced himself to do a little meditative breathing as he put the thought of his extended family aside and returned to admiring his students' gravity.

Maybe he was rubbing off on them, after three hours of acquaintance. Drew, in amused agreement with pretty much all of the other instructors, did sometimes say James took himself and his job too seriously. But James wasn't a slacker, and skiing *was* serious business. It was dangerous, first of all, at every level. Second, and this was probably why he volunteered to teach Level One, bad habits were ingrained early. It was James' job to nip all that in the bud, and in its place to promote precision, proper techniques, and good practices—all leading to clean, crisp skiing. Safety first, and the skills would follow.

Mike took off, slowly at first, then picking up a bit of speed. He was one of the best in the group, although he tended towards hairpin turns. James monitored his wedge—the shape his skis made, their tips turned together—which was stable, and kept an eye on his tails—the back ends of his skis—as he finished his final turn, coming to a slow stop at the bottom of the slope, near the line for the conveyor. Mike's final turn had been a bit fast, and he'd yanked his upper leg into position, rather than shifting his weight and letting his edges guide him through a slower turn, but there was no use in yelling this information down the slope, only to have the wind whisk it away. So, James mentioned it to the rest of the kids and made a mental note to talk to Mike about it later.

One by one, the rest of James' students made their way down the slope under his close supervision, only one of them careening out of control—and, even then, Alexis managed to recover her balance before falling. Just when James thought she'd end up running into the mesh fencing that closed off the training area, she jerked her skis together and sideways at the same time, stopping so suddenly she looked a bit wobbly. James sped down the slope toward her. When he stopped, using the same maneuver she'd performed, albeit more expertly, his long skis sprayed her short legs with snow.

"Sorry about that," he said, gesturing to the white powder that was now spread across her shins. And then, more gently, "Are you alright?"

She nodded, looking a bit pale. "What was that?"

"What you just did? That's called a hockey stop. It's pretty advanced stuff. You don't play ice hockey, by any chance, do you?"

Alexis nodded again, understanding dawning. "A little, with my big sister on the pond in our backyard."

As he'd suspected. "That means you acted on instinct. Hockey stops are important because they can help prevent collisions, but they can also be scary because they happen really fast."

"I'm not scared!" She protested, straightening in her blue and green onesie.

James nodded gravely. "I'm glad to hear it. And I'm proud of you, you handled that really well." She beamed. "Now, shall we all ski over to the lodge?" The other kids had gathered in a cluster by the fence. "If we take it slow, avoid other skiers, and remember to stay in pizza mode, we won't have to worry about hockey stops." When working with kids, the instructors tended to use food-inspired terminology. Pizza was the name for the wedge shape beginners made with their tips, which helped them control their speed. French fries meant the more advanced, parallel skiing.

"If I stay in pizza can I have hot chocolate?"

James nodded solemnly at Sarah. "Of course." He always kept his promises.

An hour later, James sat in the instructors' lounge, which was really just a fancy name for the basement of the same building that housed daycare and the ski school office. The kids had all been picked up by their parents, some of whom remembered to tip, after a long round of Disney sing-alongs and a pitcher full of instant hot chocolate made with water—because the resort wouldn't spring for milk.

"Hey, man." Drew shuffled in, his gait smooth despite his clunky boots. "You done for the day?"

"No, I've got another round with the kids this afternoon. How was Sergio?" Sergio was one of Drew's private clients, one of the many who'd followed him from Vail.

"Good! We went up the tram—the line was long but, man, the triple blacks were worth the wait." Only the most advanced skiers took the tram up to the top of the mountain, in pursuit of the triple black diamond trails and rocky chutes, as well as access to the Big Couloir.

"Was there enough snow?" Sometimes the resort had to close off access to the trickier trails, whose ski-ability depended on how much snow there was and the temperature at the top, as well as visibility. They generally wanted to avoid any rise in mortality rates, although the near-death nature of the experience didn't exactly deter the more fanatical thrill-seekers—quite the opposite. Adrenaline junkies, all of them. James understood that high, and the accompanying cravings, but he didn't seek it anymore. Not after his adolescence.

"Yeah, Thursday's storm replenished the snowpack. But I've been looking at the forecast and I'm not sure they won't have to close off some of the chutes, come midweek. It's going to be a scorcher. And you know what that means." Less snow, more rocks, ice in the morning and slush in the afternoon—typical spring skiing, made worse by climate change.

James frowned. "Still, spring break isn't over. The hordes continue to descend." He sighed. For a while there, after the winter holidays, there had been a lull in visitors to Blue Sky Resort. Weekends had remained busy, but the weeks themselves were fairly empty, leaving him plenty of time to write music and relax. The past couple of weeks, however, had seen the tranquil resort transformed into a zoo. It would be like this for the next few weeks, too. Until the end of the season, really, which was in April.

Spring break was the bane of James' existence as a ski instructor. It was worse than the winter holidays, in terms of visitors. Mostly because over Christmas and New Year's families found their way to the mountain, whereas spring break summoned not only families but packs of screaming college students who were more interested in the après, the after party, than in doing any actual skiing. They showed up in their "retro" onesies—garish recreations of '80s snow bunny styles— with their borrowed lift passes like fake IDs, not bothering with helmets and wearing ill-fitting rental skis. Little did they know, the Blue Sky après situation was mediocre at best, dire compared to exotic Courchevel or even the more local Jackson Hole.

James tried not to let his disdain for spring breakers get out of hand, but it was really frustrating when he was trying to take a group of beginners down a green only to find it clogged up by tipsy twenty-somethings. Personally, James didn't drink. He didn't do drugs at all, including caffeine—with the exception of a pot of perfectly brewed green tea, twice a day. Speaking of which...

"I'm making some tea, do you want any?"

Drew grimaced. "Not if it's that genmaicha stuff. Tastes like pond-water."

"To each his own." James bent to unbuckle his boots.

Drew sat and followed suit. "How were the kids?"

"Good, I had a good group." James eased one foot out of the tight fit, then the other, flexing his freed toes.

"You're back to adults tomorrow, right?"

James nodded, his mouth twisting into a line.

"You don't look too happy about it," Drew observed, taking in James' expression. "I thought you preferred working with adults."

"I do. I just worry."

"About?" Drew groaned as he got his left foot free, rolling out his ankle a few times.

"It's spring break. No one's going to take it seriously."

Drew laughed. "Dude, you've gotta lighten up. They pay you

either way, so have some fun! You never know what's to come. Or who." He winked, and James rolled his eyes. Drew was convinced that James' latest dry spell was soon to end. James, on the other hand, had resigned himself to a lifetime of loneliness. At least, he thought, standing up, he had his music. And his tea.

CHAPTER 2
GROUP LESSON

ESTIE FULLY WOKE up on the fourth ring of the alarm, which wailed at an evil volume until she unlocked the app by solving a simple math problem. Simple, according to the app's designation; it still took her three tries.

She felt slightly sick, which might have been the altitude, and a little… wobbly. Not to mention groggy. The grogginess might just have been the fact that she was waking up at six-thirty, but the wobbliness was due to her having changed time zones. Jet lag was a drag for most sentient creatures, but bipolar humans were especially sensitive. Estie's internal clock was off, by a lot of hours, and she could feel the disruption like she was stuck between different dimensions. Still, she'd brought enough lithium to last her the week, so the travel wasn't going to trigger a manic episode—which was possible if a person wasn't careful. And Estie *was* capable of being careful, when her life was on the line.

Dragging herself out of bed, Estie got dressed for a day on the mountain—layering long underwear over the extra long ski socks she'd borrowed from her sister. Flo wasn't as tall as Estie, but their feet were about the same size. Then she pulled her vintage onesie from her bag, popped her morning pills, and plodded downstairs. As she entered the open-plan kitchen of the rental house, she slowed, staring with wide eyes out the even wider window.

Dawn was breaking on the mountain, dyeing its white face a color like living coral. Orange—no, pink. Estie felt a kind of tug as she gazed upon the scene, as though she ought to be sitting in front of her computer, jotting down a description of the Montana morning. She shook herself. Writing would have to wait. The next four hours would be devoted to skiing—rather, the closest approximation to the activity that she, a non-athlete, could make.

"It's beautiful, isn't it?" Ben smiled up at Estie from his seat at the table. "The mountain, I mean. That's where we're going to be skiing. They call it the Lonely Peak."

Estie frowned, crossing over to the fridge. "I thought it was called Blue Sky." She rummaged for a regular yogurt, finding only the fancy Norwegian kind her sister liked. What was a cloud berry, anyway?

"The *town's* called Blue Sky, and the resort," her brother interjected, sounding a little smug. "Surprised you didn't do your research."

Estie rolled her eyes as she took her place at the table. "I reserve my research skills for my books, Freddy. Besides, why Google something when I can just ask you, the walking, talking encyclopedia?"

"Now, now, you two." Their mother emerged in long underwear patterned after the alleged ancestral tartan. She'd gotten really into DNA testing, lately, and had spent hours at a time building family trees online. Apparently, they were all quite Scottish. "Save some of that energy for the slopes."

"Oh, but Estie won't be going out on the slopes, Mom." Freddy smiled patronizingly. "She'll be stuck in the training area, since she doesn't know how to ski."

"I've got better things to do with my time," Estie sniped.

"Like what?"

A little shrilly, she replied, "Write!" She shouldn't be wasting her day, trudging around on two pieces of wood. No, wait. Not wood. What were skis made of? Fiberglass? It didn't matter, because it didn't seem easy or especially safe. Maybe it wasn't too late to back out…

"I know that look, Esther…" Her mother warned. "And I'll remind you that we already booked and paid for your lesson, so no grumbling. Besides, it'll be fun. Who knows! You might meet the love of your life."

"Yeah, then you could actually write what you know. Isn't that the first rule of writing?"

Estie leveled her brother with a look. His boyfriend, beside him, bit his lip in anticipation of a proper brawl. "Didn't you fail English, Freddy? Or did you just get a 1 on the AP?"

"Esther! That's enough, both of you! Now, finish your breakfasts or we'll be late."

They were, despite Estie's mother's cajoling, late. And there was a massive line at the rental shop, meaning that Estie had to say a hasty goodbye to her family and run—or rather, plod, in her unsecured boots, clutching her skis and poles and helmet to her chest—across the crowded valley to the training area. Hurriedly, she threw on her helmet then tossed her skis to the ground and, after bending to buckle her boots, stepped into the long, thin, twin deathtraps. Pushing off with the help of her poles, she half-slid, half-strode over to the beginner's flag, where a group of adults were clustered. Based on their body language, which alternated between apprehensive and nervous but enthusiastic, Estie judged these to be fellow students.

As she approached her presumed peers, however, Estie felt herself start to slip. The snow beneath her skis felt hard and icy and suddenly steep. Had she stumbled upon some kind of slope? Having absolutely no idea what to do or how to stop herself, and utterly terrified of falling given the horror stories she'd heard about ACLs and ankles, Estie flailed. Her arms went up, her knees gave out, and her feet flew forwards even as the rest of her fell backwards. Estie shut her eyes against the morning sky, certain that this breath would be her last. But before she could hit the ground, she found herself suspended in the air —caught in the strong arms of a stranger.

"Easy there," he murmured, steadying her with his capable hands.

Estie opened her eyes and found, to her surprise, that she was staring into a sea of green. Like the moss that lined the forest floor or filled the gaps between the roots of old trees. Green eyes, framed by long brown lashes and set above high, angular cheekbones—although these were obscured, partially, by a close-fitting black ski helmet.

Her awed gaze trailing down the stranger's face, Estie found a straight, unbroken nose leading to a pair of curved and eminently kissable lips—although why she was thinking about kissing was beyond her—framed by a lush brown mustache, the color of polished mahogany.

"Can you stand?" His voice was gentle, like a summer evening's embrace, and his calm gaze didn't waver once, even as she surveyed his face.

Estie opened her mouth to speak but no sound came out. She was afraid he could hear her heart beating, that he somehow knew the truth of her traitorous thoughts. But, then again, she didn't feel afraid at all. Not of anything, not in his arms. Which was… Well, she could think about that later.

Finally, realizing she had to respond soon or else he'd think something was wrong when really everything was right, all gloriously right, Estie stuttered a single syllable. "Y-yes."

Slowly, his hands steadying her all the while, the stranger righted Estie. He didn't let go immediately, waiting to make sure she was stable on her feet, first. He smiled slightly, and the air around Estie seemed a degree warmer, the sun a measure brighter. "Shall we get you out of those skis?"

Confused, Estie shook her head. "No, I—I'm here for the lesson."

The stranger nodded and his faint smile faded, replaced by a strange solemnity. One of his hands fell from her waist, although the other remained firm on her shoulder. "So I gathered. But we don't start the lesson on our skis."

Oh. No one had told her that. Estie started to feel the fool, the feeling increasing as she came to the realization that—"Wait, so you're the instructor?"

James gazed at the woman who'd nearly fallen, probably for a moment too long. Her eyes were a warm brown, like the coffee he didn't drink, and her hair was a gleaming, golden red—he longed to loosen her lone braid, to card his fingers through her curls, some of which had already escaped. A blush suffused her cheeks, tinging them the way dawn painted the mountain pink. Like the lone peak, with its snowy face catching the rising sun's color, she was radiant. She was a revelation. She was... his student.

"Yes." He cleared his throat. "I'm your instructor. James."

"Estie," she offered, twisting slightly in her skis.

"Right, well. Good to meet you, Estie."

A little shyly, she returned the greeting.

Shaking himself, James tore his eyes from hers, his hand from her shoulder, and reached for one of his poles to pop her out of her skis. She stepped out of them clumsily, gripping his proffered forearm with her ungloved hand—a mitten, attached by a string to the wrist of her snowsuit, dangled—and he caught a flash of electric blue nail polish. It was chipped—a little, he suspected, like her confidence.

Estie sighed and started to speak in a self-deprecating tone. "I know, I know. You don't have to comment. I look like an athlete, but I promise you, as you have just witnessed, I am not one. It's the height. It fools everyone." She was, in fact, quite tall. It was hard to say exactly how tall, given that she wore boots, but she couldn't have been less than six foot, frankly. Only a few inches shorter than he.

"I wasn't going to comment, except to tell you not to worry about it," he returned. "Everybody falls. The key is to know how to fall, so you don't hurt yourself during the descent or on impact."

Her eyes lit up, and some of the embarrassment was replaced by good humor. "Ah, but I didn't."

James felt his brows knit in confusion. "Didn't what?"

"Fall. I didn't fall. You caught me, so my record remains perfect."

He found himself smiling again, which was odd enough given how rarely he smiled these days. Then he shook his head in disbelief at her playfully competitive attitude—as well as her ability to bounce back from what could have been a humiliating start. Still, he was sure her near-fall stung a little, so he decided to steer the conversation away from sensitive waters. That, and the lesson was about to begin. "Indeed. Now, Estie, why don't you pick up your skis and we can join the others who are here for the group lesson. You're a Level One, right?"

She nodded, and that self-deprecation returned in the form of a smirk. "Couldn't you tell?"

"As I said, everybody falls."

"Except for me," she teased.

James really needed to nip this—whatever it was—in the bud and begin the lesson. But her tone was so inviting… Fortunately, one of his other students chose that moment to speak.

"Excuse me, are we in the right place?"

James turned away from Estie—which was, all in all, a surprisingly painful thing to do, like pulling a magnet away from its match—and addressed the assembled group. "Yes, if you're a Level One, according to an employee or the online assessment. This is the group for beginners. I'm your instructor, James." He looked around the small circle of students—six in all, including Estie. "Why don't you introduce yourselves, one by one—name, where you're from, level of experience, any goals for today, et cetera."

The student who'd spoken up started. His name was Tom. The rest followed, some enthusiastic, some apprehensive, few with any stated goals. Then it was Estie's turn.

She flashed that smile again, the playful one, and addressed the group. "I'm Estie, as you may have overheard. I'm from Boston, although I grew up in the suburbs, actually. I suppose that's more information than you asked for," she directed this last statement at James, who was in fact fascinated. Boston, eh? It explained her accent. "But I'm prone to oversharing, sorry! Anyway. I have skied before, as a child, but not since I was, like, ten. And I was rubbish then. Still am, for those of you who missed my spectacularly embarrassing entrance. Thanks, James, for saving me." She sent him a smaller smile, a more secretive one, and he found himself staring.

He liked the way she said his name, like they were old friends.

"I can tell, already, you're going to be a brilliant instructor. And I swear I'm not brown nosing. Well, not *just*."

She winked. She actually winked. James' heart skipped a beat.

A little gruffly, he thanked her. And tried not to dwell on the way her lips curved in answer. Then, clearing his throat, he addressed the group, several of whose members were watching Estie and him with an amused expression. Great. "Now, I see a lot of you are holding onto your skis. Well, you can toss them to the side, for now. We'll be starting on our feet."

"On our feet? I thought the whole point of this lesson was to learn how to ski." A third student, this one named... Allison, eyed him suspiciously as she held onto her teal rental skis.

"It's important to learn how to move before you actually start to move. If you know where to point your feet, how to bend your knees, and the angles that grant control and determine speed, you'll be halfway to safe, and successful, skiing. Before you've even hit the half-pipe."

A couple of the students nodded, slowly. Estie narrowed her eyes, perhaps a touch impatiently, but she'd have to learn along with everyone else that there were no safe shortcuts on the slopes. "Anything Goes" was a song written by Cole Porter, not a reliable winter sports philosophy.

James gestured to Estie's skis, which she had planted in the ground and was now leaning against. "If you'll put those down by the mesh fence, Estie?"

After fifteen minutes of footwork, during which he struggled to divide his attention equitably amongst his charges, due to the presence and playful persistence of a certain copper-haired cutie, James felt his new students were ready for their first slope, the half-pipe. There, they would learn wedges, stops, speed control, and turns.

James looked up from Tom's feet and found himself locking eyes with Estie. She smiled, her eyes bright with learning's light. And perhaps a little flirtation, too. "Gather your skis, team, and step into them." Around him, his students straightened eagerly. "We're hitting the half-pipe."

"Thanks for the lesson, James!" Estie had actually really enjoyed herself. After a half hour on the half-pipe, she'd graduated to the amusingly named Lazy River slope, where she'd worked further on her turns.

Estie's instructor looked up at her, a little intensely. "You're not staying the full day?"

She shook her head and he seemed… disappointed? Relieved? Estie couldn't tell, she didn't know him well enough to read his somewhat stoic range of expressions. But she rather thought it was a mixture of both. "I have to get back to my computer."

"Work?"

She shrugged. "Sort of. I mean, yes. I'm a writer," she explained, and his confusion faded, replaced by curiosity.

"What do you write?" James leaned on his pole, and Estie tried not to think about the body beneath the layers. Or the fact that he was asking her about herself. He was probably just being polite.

"Romance novels!" It was a risk, telling a hot guy—telling anyone—what genre she wrote in. But it was also a good litmus. For the same reason, really. A lot of people looked down on romance novels, turned their noses up at the billion dollar industry. Not that money made a genre special, or that success indicated superiority. Estie would still read and write romance regardless of whether or not it was lucrative. It was what she did, the world in which she lived. The language she spoke, or at least the one in which she wrote, wasn't English. It was love.

James' eyes widened. "You're a published author?"

"Self-published, yes."

He didn't push for her pen name, and Estie couldn't decide whether that was a relief or a disappointment. For some strange reason, that surely had nothing to do with the way he'd caught her, or how he'd held her in his arms, she wanted to share her world—worlds, rather—with him. She wanted to be brave, and bold, and open. As, to her own surprise, she had been, throughout the lesson. But she didn't want to scare him off, or overstep a professional boundary. So she just smiled, and waited for him to dismiss her and then disappear forever.

Instead, he looked her right in the eye and said, with great solemnity and something almost akin to reverence, "I imagine your novels are passionate, and intense."

Estie opened her mouth but no sound came out. *Oh dear lord,* she thought—was this what it was like? Was she going to *swoon*? "W —why?"

James was silent a moment, and then he surprised her again. "Your turns."

"My turns?"

"I imagine you write the way you ski. Passionately. With an irrepressible intensity." His expression was sincere. He wasn't taking the piss out of romance novels, or making fun of her. He was serious.

"I think—" Estie paused, just checking to make sure that this was indeed reality, "I think that's the greatest compliment I've ever received."

James chuckled. It was the first time she'd heard him laugh, despite her having spent the whole morning with him. She'd learned, over the course of the last couple hours, that he took skiing *very* seriously. Then, Estie stopped caring about skiing, or how deadly serious James could be, because her incredibly hot ski instructor had started to take off his helmet, ducking his head to do so. She was going to see his whole face! It was weird that she was this excited about it, wasn't it?

Estie didn't have time to dwell on her own oddity, however, because the helmet was now off, hanging by James' side in his ungloved hand. And Estie wished, how she wished, she'd braced herself against one of her poles. Because she wasn't ready for the vision of beauty before her.

James lifted his chin and shook out his hair, which was long and luscious and didn't look at all like it had been stuck inside a helmet for the better part of four hours. It fell in mahogany waves to the edge of his jaw, framing his frankly beautiful face, curling around the shell of his ear, as he tucked it away.

"Thank you," she said, a bit breathlessly. She wasn't sure if she was thanking him belatedly for the compliment, or for removing the impediment to her ogling. She wasn't even sure she should be thanking him, not for revealing his godlike splendor, because now, whenever she saw him wearing a helmet, all she'd be able to think about would be the sheer artistry that she couldn't see.

"You're welcome," he replied, utterly ignorant of the effect he had on her.

"Right, well. Bye, then." She sort of lifted her hand and gave a little wave.

He lifted his, free of its glove, his fingers long and and elegant in the light, and waved back, that slightly stern expression returning. "Goodbye, Estie."

Christ, but she could barely breathe.

Estie trudged back to base, feeling worse the further she went from James. She struggled to walk in her stiff boots, to carry her unwieldy skis. Her family were too busy chatting about their adventures to pay much attention to her, which was fine by Estie. She had thoughts to think. Realities to on which to reflect. Fantasies about which to, well, fantasize—freely.

James occupied the majority of her mind, his thick mustache and his eyes so kind. But, as the car pulled away from the mountain village, she began to imagine things, too. And, she realized, by the time they parked in front of the house, she had writing to do.

She stripped off her ski gear and sat down at her computer still in her sweat-dampened long underwear. The words flowed, like water from a font. She typed as quickly as she could.

As she wrote, she began to be aware of two facts: first, that her reality today had been better than any fantasy. Estie had gotten to flirt, which was fun of the highest order; to be her true and playful self, in spite of the jet lag. She'd actually started enjoying herself, once she was free of the confines of her close-knit family. But it wasn't just getting away from her family that had opened Estie up to being her authentic self, the person she was but wasn't always free to be; it was meeting that man, that handsome and capable and kind man, whose mere presence seemed to set her free to be, well... *Estie.* Put simply.

The second fact of which she had become aware was that even though Estie knew it couldn't get any better than this, than her lively and oh-so-lovely liberation, she was going to try. She was going to chase the high—beyond writing, which was only a tempting proxy for the real thing, a proxy for which she'd become all too accustomed to settling—she'd start living.

Sure, it probably wouldn't go or get her anywhere. Rather, she wouldn't let it go or get her anywhere. Estie did *not* intend to fall in love with a man she'd just met, a man she'd leave in a week—that wasn't the plan! But why should that stop her from having a little fun and flirtation? It would only be—*could* only ever be—a fling. There would be no Happily-Ever-After-ing. By Estie's own design. James, if he was interested, would simply help Estie while away the time...

CHAPTER 3
CHAIR LIFT

"Estie! You're awake." As her mother stared at her, Estie became acutely aware of the fact that she'd forgotten to braid the long, wavy mass of her hair before bed. Her head probably looked like a rat's nest.

Grimacing, she wished her mother a good morning. "Is there food?"

"Your father's making eggs in the kitchen. But what are you doing up?"

It *was* only seven. An ungodly hour. "I'm gonna do another day of lessons," Estie explained. "A full day, this time."

"Oh, how nice!" Estie's mother's smile shrank into a sterner twist of the lips. "But you'd better eat quick! We leave in thirty minutes and we're *not* going to be late, again."

Estie nodded and headed downstairs to the kitchen, where everybody stared. "Is it my hair?" Estie asked, in a bored tone that belied her anxiety—she felt jet lagged and jittery despite not yet having had any coffee.

"No," her sister assured her. "We just weren't expecting you."

"Are you joining us today?" Her father asked, passing her a plate full of bacon and eggs before digging into his own breakfast.

"No, but I am going to do another day of ski school." She bit down on the bacon, which was possibly the best thing she'd ever tasted, and let out an appreciative groan.

"Why?" Miles frowned in confusion. "I thought you hated skiing."

Freddy grinned from across the kitchen table. "Maybe her instructor's hot and she just wants to 'spend time' with him."

Her cheeks aflame, Estie chucked a piece of burnt bacon at her brother's head. "Fuck off, Frederick. I just…" Taking a bite of her eggs, she struggled to come up with a plausible explanation. Something a bit more family-friendly than the truth, which was that she was incredibly, and unprecedentedly, aware of and aroused by another human. "I just think I might like to learn to ski. You know, it could be… useful. Or fun. You enjoy it, don't you?" She directed this last question at Freddy.

"Yeah, but I'm actually good at it—"

She narrowed her eyes, swallowed, and smiled bitterly. "Tell me, Ben, how do you make room in your relationship with my brother for his enormous ego? Must be a tight squeeze."

Ben raised his hands preventatively. "Do not drag me into this, Estie."

Estie's mother, who had followed her daughter downstairs, chose this moment to interject. "Well, I think it's swell."

Freddy scoffed. "Swell?"

"I think it's nice that your sister wants to broaden her horizons! Besides, this way she won't be bored."

"*She* is still in the room and *she* wouldn't be bored if her family hadn't dragged her two thirds of the way across the country…"

Her mother patted her hand affectionately. "Yes, dear. It's all your father's fault for suggesting this ski holiday in the first place."

Estie's father looked up from his scrambled eggs. "What? What did I do?"

"Nothing, Dad." Estie sighed, then forced a smile. Except, she didn't even have to force it. The idea of spending another day with James had her giddy with anticipation. "So, yeah." She scarfed down the rest of her eggs. "I'm gonna go get dressed. Can whatever car I'm in leave early, so I can renew my rental skis?"

Flo nodded. "Yeah, Miles and I will take you. We wanted to hit the slopes before the spring breakers, anyway. Trying to avoid the inevitable the tram line." She rolled her eyes, then glanced at their mother. "Mom, you okay to drive with Dad, Ben, and Freddy?"

She laughed. "Just me and my boys." She sent Estie's brother-in-law-to-be a sweet smile. "Minus Miles, of course. You know I love you, Miles."

Flo squeezed her fiancé's free hand. "Not as much as *I* love you."

Estie sighed. Was it any wonder she wrote romance, surrounded as she was by such love? Still, it would be nice to have her own story, her own someone to have and to hold during the long days and all through the night. She'd work on finding love, once she got back to boring old Boston. For now, though, there was sex. Or, at the very least, flirtation.

"Alright, I'll be ready in five. Don't leave without me!" She pushed back from the table, crossed over into the kitchen, and loaded her scraped plate into the dishwasher.

Watching her little sister impassively, but without having relinquished her fiancé's fingers, Flo took a sip of her coffee. "Wouldn't dream of it, sis."

James downed the last dregs of his tea, then quickly washed the cup and set it to dry. He emptied the pot of its leached leaves, tipping them into the compost container he kept by the door, and then rinsed it and set it on the drying rack.

"Are you ready?" His roommate had yet to surface from the bedroom they shared—due to the high cost and limited availability of seasonal housing, more than any desire to spend that much time together.

As James did one last sweep of the kitchen, however, to make sure all dishes were put away, Drew emerged. He was already wearing his regulation snow pants and jacket—both a bright cerulean with the Blue Sky Resort logo, to more easily identify him as an instructor. "Yeah, my gear's in the car. I put yours in last night, too."

"Thank you." James dried his hands on a dishtowel that had been embroidered with blue-violet mountain cornflowers, *centaurea montana* —a going away gift from his mother, who loved nothing more than needlework, except perhaps botany.

James grabbed his keys and phone and made for the door, Drew following. After grabbing their boots, they locked the apartment behind them and piled into James' beat up but surprisingly fuel efficient, truck.

"You teaching Level One again today?"

James nodded, eyes on the road.

"How was it, yesterday? I know you were worried—"

"It was fine." It had been more than fine. It had been fun, thanks to the welcome warmth and irrepressible humor of one young woman. Student, he reminded himself. Estie was his student.

"Taciturn today, eh?"

James glanced over at Drew, who was grinning at him. "No, it's just seven in the morning. I'm tired."

"Anything to do with your tossing and turning all night?"

"What?"

Drew laughed. "You were talking in your sleep again, man."

Shit. "What did I say?" James tried to keep his curiosity sounding casual, but the question came out too quickly.

"Why? Worried you let slip some secrets?" Drew chuckled. "You did keep talking about her hair."

Shit shit shit. "What?" James feigned confusion. But the answer was obvious. He'd been dreaming of Estie, of loosening her long copper plait. He didn't remember it, but it was the only logical conclusion.

"I dunno, man. You didn't name names, you just mumbled a bit about some chick. Honestly, most of it was unintelligible." Drew shot James a curious look. "Have you started seeing someone?"

"No," James answered, a half-second too soon. "You know I don't mix with fellow instructors, and the locals have too much disdain for seasonals to actually acknowledge any of us as sexual prospects."

"That's not true," Drew protested. "I hooked up with Cassie, and she's a lifelong resident of Blue Sky."

"Yeah, and are you still with her?"

Drew frowned. "It was a mutual understanding, man. We're all adults, here."

"Whatever." James searched for another subject. "What are you teaching today? Or should I say 'whom?'"

Laughing, Drew fiddled with the radio. "Private, with Lindsay. And you should say 'who' like a normal twenty-four-year-old."

Lindsay was one of Drew's regulars. "I'm not going to compromise my grammar simply because it has become unfashionable to speak well."

Drew sighed airily. "I look forward to the day when some girl pulls the stick out of your ass. Or, possibly, puts one in."

Blushing, James turned the dial up on the radio. Dolly Parton's cheery vocals swelled forth from the stereo as they pulled into the employee lot. Drew tumbled out of the truck and retrieved his skis, poles, boots, and helmet from the back. James did the same, with slightly more dignity, and then he locked the car. Together, hefting their gear over their shoulders, they made the long trek to the village at the base of the mountain.

The employee locker rooms were a zoo, and James lost track of Drew as the two of them made their way through. Sitting down on a crowded bench, James shucked his shoes and started the perennially awkward process of putting on his ski boots.

By nine, the employees had all been briefed and the lifts had all been set to run. James' assignment was as his supervisor had promised. He was teaching Level One, again. It was good to repeat instructors over the course of a couple days. It allowed instructors to really get into a groove with their teaching while helping students retain a set of skills—as well as a sense of confidence.

All that remained true, but today all James could think about was whether or not Estie would return. Probably not, he decided, as he trudged upstairs in his heavy boots. She'd only taken the lesson to appease her family, she'd confided in him early on. She had romance novels to write—and surely her career took precedence over a hobby that had been thrust upon her by her more athletically-inclined family members.

Confident that he wouldn't catch a glimpse of her long copper plait, or the mischievous curve of her pretty pink lips, James stepped out into the sunshine—and stopped dead in his tracks.

Ten feet away, Estie leaned against her propped up skis, watching the passersby. Presumably hearing the crunch of his boots against the snow, she whipped her head around as he approached.

"James!" Her face brightened considerably. "I was hoping you'd be here again today."

James tried not to think about the fact that she'd been thinking about him. She probably hadn't—saying that was probably just her way of being polite. As such, he made an effort to repress any playfulness in his tone. Even though there was something about her that made him want to, well, play. "Well, Estie, I do work here."

"Mmm, true. I wonder what wicked things you've done in life to deserve being stuck teaching me."

"It's no trial, to teach you." He meant it, too. Estie was a pleasure to teach. She was clumsy, true, but she took direction well, and she actually took skiing quite seriously, to his surprise. And yet, she was also fun and funny and playful. She rose to every occasion with good humor and no small amount of grace. James wanted to tell her all of that, to dispel any notion she might have of her being a burden. But it wouldn't have been appropriate, to lavish her with praise like that. Even if it wasn't so much praise as objective fact.

James was saved from Estie's response, which would without a doubt have been flirtatious, by the arrival of the rest of the group. It wasn't that he minded Estie's flirty comments, her friendly teasing—if anything, he enjoyed it too much. She was so easy to talk to—or not talk to. Her silence was companionable, as well as her conversation. Estie made James feel comfortable in his skin, which wasn't rare, necessarily, but it was strange, because he rarely felt like that in the presence of another person. Especially not one he'd known for a single day.

"Hi, James!" A chorus of greetings met his ears, and James turned away from Estie, with equal reluctance and relief, to find the other five Level Ones. Four, actually. It appeared they'd lost one.

"Hi, all. Has anyone seen April?"

A middle-aged man named Ken, who looked remarkably like the doll James had given his little cousin for her sixth birthday, nodded. "They're taking the day off, today. Their wife's not feeling well."

"That's a pity," James remarked, sincerely. He'd liked having April in the group. They were a quiet, calm kind of person. The polar oppo-site of Estie, who sparkled and shone like his own personal sun. Well, not *his* own personal sun. James mentally chastised himself for thinking about her that way.

She wasn't for him. She didn't want him. She might flirt, but that was just her nature. Well, sometimes. He hadn't seen her flirt with the other students. But maybe he had been too focused on their form to notice. Regardless. She was flirtatious and flippant and fun—unlike anyone he knew. Unlike James, too. She didn't want him, not like that. And he couldn't want her—that was that.

After the group had spent an hour in the training area, practicing their wedges and turns, and then another half hour going up the big Magic Carpet and learning j-stops on the lower slope of an easy green, James announced that they'd be traversing over to the little chair lift that led up the far side of the mountain.

"The j-stops we just practiced will serve you well on a steeper slope," he added.

"Are you sure we're ready for this, James?" Estie couldn't help but feel very nervous. She was scared of chair lifts, which came around the corner far too fast, and she wasn't at all convinced she was ready to ski down an actual, entire trail—green or any other hue. She felt fear trickle down her spine like ice water, threatening to flood and freeze her limbs.

James turned his full attention on her. His eyes were bright, like a new leaf unfurling in spring. "Do you trust me, Estie?"

She answered immediately, surprising herself slightly. "Yes."

"Then believe me when I tell you that you are more than ready for this. That you have proven yourself capable of this."

Estie swallowed, suddenly finding it a bit hard to breath. "Oh."

He smiled, just a twitch of his mustache at the corner of his lips. But it was true, and Estie felt its warmth suffuse her soul. This attraction was beyond anything she'd ever experienced. She felt... whole? "*You* can do this."

"Alright, then. I can do this." Estie paused, a little embarrassed by her next request, which she'd swear in a court of law was not just some shameless attempt to spend time with him. "Will you sit with me, on the chair lift? I—I have an aversion to them." His brows rose. Quickly, she explained about the time she'd fallen off of one, aged seven. "I was fine, but I didn't ski the whole rest of the year, I was so scared. Still am, honestly." Estie shrugged helplessly, avoiding James' eyes.

"Of course," he said, simply. "And I'm sorry—that must have been terrifying."

She braved a glance at him, then. His eyes were wide with understanding, with concern. "It was, but I think... I think it won't be so bad, this time—if you're there with me." To her surprise, Estie found she wasn't even flirting. She meant it.

James smiled at her, then, a gentle yet generous curve of his lips. "Of course, Estie." Addressing the group at large, he beckoned to the path that cut horizontally across two runs. "Come on, everyone. Stay in line behind me as we traverse."

Tom piped up, then. "Can you go over traversing again? Just, briefly?"

"Of course." James looked around to make sure everyone was listening before starting to explain again. "Traversing is a bit like cross-country skiing. Do you remember the footwork we practiced, climbing up and down the half-pipe?"

Tom nodded. Estie bit her lip.

"It's that, only you'll be moving forward across the slope, not up or down. Bend your knees, *don't* point your skis up or downhill, because that will cause you to slip, and really try to work those edges. And be aware of your surroundings!" He glanced around the group again. "If someone is coming down in your direction and you're scared that they're going to hit you, *keep moving*. If you stop, you're far more likely to cause a crash."

With that warning, James beckoned for them to begin. In the end, no one crashed—although Ken came close—and after five minutes of pulling themselves across the wide open slope, the group found themselves in line for the chair lift. True to his word, James skied into place beside Estie. When it was their turn, he even had the operator slow the lift so that she could ease into position. Estie was genuinely moved by his kindness, his consideration. So moved that she forgot her fear long enough to let the lift scoop them both up.

As soon as they were in the air, James drew the safety bar down. Estie's skis hung heavy, knocking into James', and she was scared they'd fall off—or, worse, that she'd be dragged down with them.

"Sorry!"

"Don't worry about." He made no move to avoid her, however, even as her right leg pressed against his left.

"Sorry about *all* of that. The chair lift stuff. I'm a bit of a scaredy-cat," she confessed, too embarrassed and uncomfortable to even think about the heat of his thigh against hers. Well, not entirely. Something about James made her feel safe, and free of judgment. She found herself confiding in him—confessing, not that her diagnosis was a sin: "It's probably the bipolar. Makes me feel things more strongly, including fear. Although it could also be the anxiety."

James shook his head, his expression unreadable as his face was largely obscured by his goggles. His voice, however, was full of warmth. "You put safety first. There's nothing wrong with that. Especially when it's critical to your wellbeing. Besides, it's better than being a stick-in-the-mud."

The ironic note on which he finished, and the ease with which he accepted her diagnosis, startled a laugh out of her. "Is that what your friends call you?"

His voice was dark and deep when he answered, "Yes."

"It's not terribly nice of them. You take life seriously. Isn't that a good thing?"

"I think it is, but I seem to be alone in that department."

Estie smiled, a little shyly given that she'd been going for flirtatious. "You're not alone. You have me."

He gazed at her for a long minute without speaking, and Estie's words seemed to linger, long past the point when they should have been carried away by the breeze. She meant them, she realized, belatedly. Meant them more than she'd meant to mean them…

Finally, after Estie had tried and failed to make sense of what she was feeling, James cleared his throat. "So, you're a writer?"

She laughed lightly, a little relieved by the change in conversational tack. "We've covered this."

"Right. Of course." He nodded—nervously, it seemed. But what did he have to be nervous about? He wasn't scared of heights, and he didn't seem to have been suddenly consumed by a kind of transcendent desire that he had never felt before, and couldn't even name. "I— I'm a bit of a writer, too."

"Really?" Estie allowed herself to be distracted by curiosity. "What do you write?"

"Songs," he said simply, then specified, "love songs."

Estie gazed at him in awe. "Love songs?"

He nodded, his mustache twitching with something akin to anxiety. "Mostly."

"That's brilliant! I could never write lyrics, much less music to go with them." Estie shook her head sadly. Then she perked up again, full of questions. "What kind of instrument do you play?"

He pulled off his glove and offered her his hand. She was mesmerized by the length of his fingers, the sloping valley of his palm, the ridges that were callouses, even the little scars. "Guitar, mostly, as you can see. And I sing. I taught myself to play the drums, too, and the piano. Even the banjo, when there's one for me to borrow."

Her fear forgotten, Estie was instead amazed. James blushed faintly when she told him so. Or perhaps it was just the cold, coloring his cheeks. "Do you perform, ever?"

"Not my own compositions, but covers, yes." He looked out over the trees, into the distance. "There's a small bar in town, few but the locals know it. They call it the Little Couloir. I play there, some nights, for the contents of the tip jar."

Estie sighed, feeling dreamy. "I wish you'd play for me." She hadn't meant to say it, but the truth had just sort of slipped out.

James cocked his head and Estie got the sense that he saw beyond the surface of her. Feeling her cheeks heat, she looked away. "Maybe I will," he said, simply. Then, raising his voice over the whistling wind, he asked, "When were you diagnosed?"

Surprised, Estie turned back to him. "With bipolar disorder? When I was a teenager. I got really manic, applying for colleges. I wrote like ten personal essays." His brow furrowed; he'd probably long since forgotten or repressed the Herculean labor that was the college application process. "You're only supposed to write one."

He watched her for a moment. Estie wished she could see his face, in full. Her fingers curled around the cold bar, eager to tug off his heavy helmet, let it fall into the forest below. "Were any of them any good?"

"No—I can't write well, when I'm manic. Depressed, yes—barely. But manic... I just lose control, and there's no internal logic, no order—no sense, really."

James nodded thoughtfully. "When you wrote all those essays—did you know you wanted to be a writer?"

Estie almost laughed. "Oh, no! I thought I was going to go into politics or something equally insidious. No, I just got really high on stimulants—I was misdiagnosed with ADHD, which happens a *lot* to bipolar teenagers, apparently, and it led to my having a wee bit of a problem with pills—and then I cranked all ten of the essays out over the course of like three sleepless days. The third day, after I'd gone through a month's worth of meds, I thought I was having a heart attack, which is why we went to the hospital, which is how I found out I was manic, in the end. Shouldn't have been a surprise, considering how crazy my extended family is."

He didn't laugh, as someone else might have, despite her light-hearted tone. She wouldn't have minded if he'd laughed. But he didn't. Instead, frowning at his feet, he quietly confessed, "I had a stimulant problem when I was a teenager, too."

"Oh?" Estie tried not to let her surprise show.

James nodded, his brow once again furrowed. "I won't bore you with the details, but I got clean by the time I was twenty. After a close friend was hospitalized."

"For an overdose?" Estie suppressed a shiver that had nothing to do with the cold.

"No, our supply was laced with some powerful synthetics. By then, we were a couple years deep, and we'd wandered away from the prescription pills. Street drugs were cheaper."

"So I've heard." Estie bit her lip. "I'm impressed you were able to get off of them; I know how addictive uppers can be."

He nodded solemnly. "It's trite, but music saved me. Continues to do so."

Estie hummed her agreement, staring out at the snowy trails below. "Writing saved me. In the psych ward—and I wasn't there for long, just long enough to stabilize and get started on an accurate diagnosis—I used to write short stories. They were really crummy, but by the time I got out I'd learned a thing or two about discipline and creativity. Now, I write to make money, sure, and because I love it, absolutely, but mostly I write because I have to. I write to stay sane."

"I bet they weren't crummy at all," he said, quietly. They turned to look at each other. "I bet they were brilliant."

And just like that, Estie once more struggled to breathe. "I still have them, if you ever want to read them," she offered, her voice a whisper above the breeze.

James smiled beneath his now frosted mustache, a small and cautious curve of his lips. "I'd like that."

"Oh, let's talk about something lighter, shall we?" Estie laughed, and James, for the second time in the history of their acquaintance, joined in. It was cathartic, this release, this sharing of herself and her life and her not-quite-but-sort-of secrets. But it was also confusing, and complex, and Estie needed a breather. She'd only ever expected to flirt with the man, after all. Not bare her soul. "What's your favorite TV show?"

He frowned, thoughtfully. "I don't really watch television. But I do like those PBS/BBC adaptations of books."

"Period dramas?" Estie stared at James. "You're into period dramas?"

"Why, are you not?" He sounded slightly defensive.

"No," she laughed, "I am. I just... I expected you to say nature documentaries, or something."

"Actually, speaking of documentaries, I recently watched a really interesting one on the deleterious effect of the British Empire on muslin production in India."

Estie beamed—not because there was anything good about the

British Empire, but rather because it felt so fantastic to hear James speak on a subject about which he was enthusiastic. A subject that wasn't skiing. "Tell me about it, James."

He launched into a detailed introduction. They talked and talked, their thighs pressed against each other, their skis knocking about in the breeze, until there was no time left to talk. Until the chair lift set them down and Estie slid into the little valley below the lift's exit to meet her waiting peers. She hadn't realized just how intimate a ride on the chair lift could be.

Estie gradually forgot how high up the mountain they were, and how nervous she'd been. Because with James, she felt safe. The safest she'd ever been. But how could someone so serious, so studious, ever have time for a frivolous person like her? And what was this, this thing between them, if it wasn't mere flirtation?

CHAPTER 4
THE LITTLE COULOIR

"DUDE, we're gonna be late. Put that away."

James answered his roommate without looking up from his journal. "I'm taking the day off."

Drew paused in the middle of pulling on his boots. "Does Eric know?"

"No, I'm looking to get fired."

"What?"

James sighed and set down his pencil. "It was a joke, Drew. Eric knows."

Drew shook his head, smiling. "I never can tell when you're kidding. It's that flat tone."

"Would you prefer I fake it?" He switched into a pleasanter, slightly higher pitch. "Use my private client voice?" Except, a little voice in the back of his head reminded him, he hadn't used that voice with Estie.

"Nah, I like that you keep me on my toes."

James picked up his pencil. "Go on, you'll be late."

Drew nodded, opening the door. Immediately, it seemed, the temperature in their apartment dropped ten degrees. But James was accustomed to the cold. "Catch you on the flip."

James nodded, returning his attention to the blank pages below. "Be safe."

Drew grinned; James didn't see it, but he heard it in his friend's voice. "Bullshit."

And then Drew was gone, the door closed behind him, shutting out the early morning light—not that there was much of it, yet. Instructors had to rise before the sun, if they wanted to beat their clients to the slopes. James could have slept in this morning—most of his peers would have, on a day off—but he didn't like to waste the day, or sully his sleep schedule by even an hour. Besides, he had songs to write. Songs he would one day sing, himself. As a teenager, he'd thought he'd be a songwriter. Behind the scenes, anonymous. But as he grew into himself, he began to realize that there was no shame in wanting some of the spotlight, too. Especially not when he knew he could sing as well as at least the worst performer on his truck's radio.

Lately, though, James had been struggling to find inspiration. Time, too, was in short supply, what with the late-season boom, courtesy of spring breakers. He thought about the past two days, the students he'd had. Well, if he were being honest with himself, his thoughts were entirely devoted to one person in particular.

Estie.

Of the warm brown eyes and the copper wisps that, curling, sprang free of her long plait over the course of the day. He shouldn't be thinking about her, not the way that he was, and the dreams—well, whatever his dreams, which were dissipating like the dew, it wasn't going to happen. Ethically, it definitely shouldn't happen. At least, not until she was no longer his student. And by then she'd be gone, back home to Boston, and he'd be another flirtation she'd forgotten.

Still, Drew remained convinced that James' creative dry spell was somehow connected to his sexual dry spell. What Drew didn't understand, however, being a more base creature, was that getting laid wouldn't help James write a love song. And that was his specialty—love songs. James wrote all kinds of songs, about life on the road and the way daybreak lit up the mountain, but what he aspired to write, above all, were songs about love so profound they made the pulse quicken, the heart pound.

The problem was that James hadn't been in love in a long time. And he refused to use lyrics to lie. Still, he was hardly going to find love in Blue Sky. He'd met every instructor, felt the spark of love with exactly none. He'd gotten to know the locals, too, performing at the smaller of the two bars in town. And the people that showed up at the resort to ski—well, he was hardly in a position to socialize. Besides, they were all rich and out of touch with reality. They wouldn't understand him, and he wouldn't understand them. And there couldn't be love without mutual understanding.

Maybe in the summer, when he returned to Maine to teach sailing on a small island midcoast, the only place he'd been able to find a job after leaving college and committing to the seasonal lifestyle, maybe he'd find someone there. It was unlikely, though, given that he knew everyone already and hadn't felt a spark yet, not in all the summers he'd worked there. Not like he had with Estie…

James frowned. He shouldn't be thinking these thoughts. It wasn't right. And it wasn't realistic. He'd find someone someday. Just not now. Feeling a faint pang of loneliness, James glared down at the blank page in front of him. So much for a morning of song writing. He might as well make that tea—or better yet, go for a run. Cardio always got him going. Got his mind off his aching heart.

In the bedroom he shared with Drew, because seasonal housing was a scam, James pulled on a pair of running leggings and an employees-only blue quarter zip. He'd be cold, at first, but he'd warm up quick. Quicker, if he let himself think of Estie…

Crossing back into the open-plan kitchen that doubled as a living room, he slipped into his sneakers, tying them with a double knot, as was his wont. James ran without music, lest he be hit by a car headed to the mountain, but he took his phone in case of emergency. It was too early in the season to carry bear spray, however, so he left the canister in the kitchen.

He stepped out of the apartment and onto the sidewalk, where he stretched for a few minutes before breaking into a jog. As an instructor, he relied upon his body for a living, so it was important for him to oil the machine. Making his way out of town and onto the backroads, James began to pick up speed. The wind on his face, whistling in his ears, he ran as though he could outrun the heartache, the loneliness, the boredom he felt—he ran as though he could replace it all with adrenaline and endorphins, and still be satisfied. It almost worked, although maybe he should have hit the slopes, gotten a hit of that Rocky Mountain high.

It wouldn't compare, though, to the way *she* made him feel. Which was why he'd taken the day off, wasn't it? The warmth with which she suffused him—it wasn't worth the risk. He wasn't avoiding Estie, per se, but he thought it might be safer to take a day. He hadn't planned on its being this painful, though.

"I'll be down in a second!" Estie cried as she contorted her face to better apply her eyeliner. She hadn't worn make up yet, in all the time she'd been in Blue Sky, for fear that she would sweat it off while skiing. But tonight they were going out on the town, all of them, and a slightly less natural look seemed appropriate. At least, that's what she'd told Flo. The truth was, it was a Hail Mary—in case she ran into James. The man had been absent from ski school all morning and all afternoon, whereas she'd been on the mountain, in search of him, forced to endure a full day of lessons without him. It had felt wrong, to ski without him. To be without him.

"Don't you want to borrow my shirt?" Flo asked, through the bathroom door.

Right. The plaid shirt. Because they were trying to "fit in." Rather, Freddy and Flo loved a theme. Although they had neglected to inform Estie of their uninspired choice ("country, Estie—think cowboys") so she hadn't packed anything for the occasion and was now forced to borrow the shirt that Flo hadn't thought fashionable enough to wear herself.

Whatever.

Estie opened the door and held out her hand, into which her sister deposited a plaid bundle.

"Cute bra," Flo commented. "See you downstairs in two?"

"Yeah, let me just put on some mascara."

Flo smirked. "Don't forget the shirt."

Estie rolled her eyes. "Yes, obviously that was implied. Wouldn't want to scandalize."

Her sister started to turn, then stopped. "Are you leaving your hair down?"

"Yeah, why?" Estie looked in the mirror. Her hair was cooperating, for once, the loose curls falling into place with the help of a hairdryer and some leave-in conditioner. "Would it look better up?"

"No, I like it down. And he will, too."

Estie froze. "Who?"

"Whoever you're trying to impress." Flo smiled, not unkindly. "Estie, you can't hide these things from me. Just be glad I haven't told Freddy."

Of course Flo had figured it out. She was observant, for a largely absent older sister. "Right, well, please don't." She slipped her arms into the plaid shirt and set to work on its buttons.

"Your secret's safe with me. Just… who is he? Someone you met in ski school, I can only assume."

Estie grimaced, rolling up the long sleeves of the borrowed shirt. "Something like that."

Flo nodded, her expression thoughtful.

"How did you know?"

Flo's smirk returned. "It's the only reason you'd return to ski school, given how much you clearly hate skiing."

"I don't hate—"

Flo lifted an eyebrow and Estie swallowed her protest.

"What is?"

"Love, or some approximation of the sensation," Flo stated, simply, then flashed Estie a smile and started down the stairs. "Two minutes!"

Love? Estie didn't know about that. She was chasing a high, embarking on a flirtation. If her efforts were rewarded with anything, it would be a fling. Just something to get her through the end of the week. And then it would end, and then the butterflies in her belly would migrate, leaving her in peace.

After a two hour, multi-course dinner at a local restaurant known for its elk and venison, they wound their way through town in search of the local dive. There was a line around the block and, Freddy discovered when he tried to talk his way in, they were charging for entry.

Estie's father frowned. "Kids, I hate to say this, but I think we might need to reevaluate our plans."

"Relax, Dad." Freddy waved their father's worry away. "It's just a little wait. They'll let us in soon, I'm sure"

Flo crossed her arms. "Are you sure? Because according to the group in front of us, the bar's at capacity and they're only letting new people in when current patrons leave." She gestured to the length of the line. "A lot of people are going to have to leave for us to get in."

Freddy groaned. "But I wanted us to go out after dinner tonight! I'm bored of sitting around, watching basketball."

"There isn't any basketball on tonight," Miles returned, "and that was a Final Four game."

"Whatever," said Freddy dismissively. "I want a night out. And so does Ben, he's just too polite to complain."

Estie's mother frowned. "Is there another bar in town?"

"Not that I'm aware of," Flo replied, with a sigh.

"I think I know a place," Estie ventured, a little shyly.

Without bothering to disguise their surprise, the rest of the group turned to her.

Freddy stared. "*Our Estie's* got the inside scoop? Is this what they teach you in ski school?"

She shrugged. "It's just something someone mentioned, in passing. A place only the locals know."

Flo uncrossed her arms. "Well, we might as well try it. Can't be any busier than this."

The so-called Little Couloir wasn't busy at all. A few blocks off the beaten path, out back behind the artisanal soap and candle store, its entrance was an unassuming metal door with a flickering sign that simply read "BAR."

Estie's father held open the door for her—this was her adventure, he had said, so it only seemed fair that she go in first. Estie was not appreciative of the gesture. Summoning her courage, however, she made to step inside. But before she could, the sound of a guitar, softly strummed, wafted out. It was followed by a familiar voice, made unfamiliar by the fact that it was raised in song. Estie froze on the threshold.

James.

He hadn't been teaching today. She'd missed him, more than she cared to admit. And now, well, here he was. Crooning a cover of Randy Travis' "Forever And Ever, Amen," a lyrical country love song that even Estie recognized.

"Estie," Freddy hissed. "Move!"

Steeling herself against the sweetest sound she'd ever heard, Estie stepped inside the little bar. It was like walking into a dream. To her left, a bartender served a line of locals. To her right, tables and chairs cluttered the space. But between them, it seemed, a narrow path had opened for her, leading directly to the man whose memory had haunted her all day.

Estie walked deeper into the bar, stopping a few feet from the stage, which was lit by a lone spotlight. If her family followed her, she didn't notice. She was too absorbed by James' stripped down performance. As he started the chorus up again, folks began to sing along. Smiling, he lifted his head.

Their eyes met, and his widened. But he held her gaze and did not look away. Not even as the crowd fell silent and he concluded the serenade, singing prayer-like promises of an everlasting love.

Apparently, the song was the last in the set, because James stood as soon as he had finished it and, after ducking his head in bashful acknowledgment of well-deserved applause, stepped forward —toward her.

"Estie." His tone was polite but his expression was inscrutable, and despite the intensity of his earlier stare she found herself doubting everything—doubting, even, her right to doubt anything.

The seconds stretched until she spoke, straining the song's spell. "I'm so sorry—I hope we're not intruding."

"You aren't. Not in the least."

Silence fell between them, like snow during the night. He seemed to be waiting for her to do something, to say something. But what? What could she say to that, not knowing if it was common courtesy or something more?

His eyes—a bright emerald in the glare of the lone spotlight, his pupils pinpricks and his irises wide—flicked from her to her family, who were waiting behind her, expectantly.

"Oh! Right, sorry." For a minute there, her family had faded, along with the bartender and the row of regulars, as Estie stood with James in the small circle of light, staring into those rare green eyes. "James, this is my family. Family, this is James. My instructor."

It felt like a lie—of omission, or something. But it was the naked truth. He was her ski instructor. No more, no less.

"*This* is your ski instructor?" Out of the corner of her eye, Estie watched Freddy's jaw drop.

Flo, too, looked surprised. But amused. She stretched out a hand. "I'm Florence, Estie's older sister. This is my fiancé, Miles." The men exchanged nods.

"And I'm Freddy, Estie's brother. Younger—but only in years." Freddy flashed James a friendly smile, just south of flirtatious. Estie very nearly rolled her eyes. "Ben here is my boyfriend." Freddy turned to Ben. "Say hi, Benji!" Ben waved a warm hello.

James returned it, then turned to Estie's mother and father, who were hanging back in a blatant attempt to allow the young people to socialize, unimpeded by the presence of their elders. "You must be Estie's parents," he surmised.

Beaming, Estie's mother nodded. "James, it's a pleasure to meet you." She nudged Estie's father. "Isn't it, darling?"

He nodded. "It's good to know my daughter's in capable hands."

Estie's gaze traveled down to where James held his guitar, cradling the instrument with obvious care. Her eyes lingered on his long fingers, his knuckles like a low mountain ridge. She'd felt those hands on her once, when he'd caught her that first day. But there had been layers between them then: snow gear, long underwear, gloves. What would it feel like to be held by him now, nothing but a borrowed shirt between those guitar string calluses and her bare skin?

"Estie?"

She snapped to attention, flushing slightly at her fevered imaginings. "What?"

Flo smiled knowingly. "Mom and Dad are going to pull those two tables together so we can sit, while the rest of us acquire some much needed alcohol. You want anything?"

Estie nodded, a little absently. "A stout, if they have one. Local would be nice but Guinness is fine."

"James, you want anything? Drinks are on us."

James shook his head resolutely. "No, but thank you." He glanced at Estie. "I don't drink."

Flo nodded and made for the bar, where the others were waiting, but Estie turned to face James more fully. "At all?"

He shrugged. "At all."

Suddenly it clicked together: he hadn't just gotten off uppers; he'd gotten sober, as well as clean. "Sorry, I shouldn't pry."

"No, it's alright. I don't mind."

Estie cocked her head. "You don't mind when a student asks you a personal question?"

"You already know the answer to that question. Besides…" He was silent for a long moment, watching the bartender pull a pint. Then he turned his eyes on her and, with a strange solemnity, he said, "You're only my student when we're on the slopes, between the hours of nine and four."

"So, I'm not your student now?" Estie was aware she was treading a treacherous trail. But she felt compelled to follow him down it, or perhaps she was the one leading them into the unknown.

He shook his head again, shifting the guitar in his hands.

His silence, his steady stare stole her breath away. Half-whispering, she dared to ask, "What am I, then? Now, to you?"

His mouth opened but no sound came out. The air between them seemed charged with something stronger than electricity. At that moment, however, Freddy arrived with Estie's beer, and it was like a switch had been flipped.

James straightened, clearing his throat. "I'd best be going," he announced, his eyes studiously avoiding Estie's. "Early morning, and all that."

Freddy nodded. "That's a shame. I bet you've got some good stories to tell about our Estie."

James shook his head. "She's an excellent student. She's progressed enormously over the past few days. I didn't teach her today, as it was my day off, but…" He turned his head to look directly at her. "I wish I had."

And in that moment, after that comment and their eyes' meeting, all doubt disappeared and Estie knew. She just knew. It wasn't politeness. It wasn't kindness. It was a connection, a real connection. He reciprocated, to some extent—and she'd take any extent—her feelings for him. And she knew, too, that she had to seize the moment. If not the moment, because he was leaving, then the day. Tomorrow. Tonight, she was with her family. Tonight, he was tired. But tomorrow, they'd meet. She'd make sure of it. And then, together, they could figure out and face whatever it was that lay between them, that connected them to each other, like Rochester's fateful string.

They said their farewells, and Estie watched James walk into the night with a new perspective, a new appreciation, a new mission.

She wouldn't be alone, always. And, if she did die alone, it wouldn't be sad and she wouldn't be sorry. Because she might not have a shot at forever and ever love—the distance between Montana and Massachusetts put a bit of a damper on this fling with James going anywhere—but a fling, a flirtation with him, would still satisfy her hungry heart.

CHAPTER 5
PRIVATE LESSON

"Oy, Heron."

At the sound of his last name, James turned to find his supervisor, sitting behind one of the desks that cluttered the resort's snow sports office, eyeing him. "Yeah, Eric?"

Eric clicked the mouse in his hand a couple times. "You've got a request for a private, half-day lesson."

James perked up immediately. Private lessons paid twice as much as groups, plus they afforded the instructor more time and attention to bestow upon a single student. Private lessons were the best way to learn, the best way to teach. But for James, given his limited client list, they were usually out of reach. "Who's the client?"

"Her name is…" Eric glanced at the computer screen, "Esther."

James' heart stuttered. *Estie.* The romance novelist with the athletic family. The woman who was brave enough to put aside her fear of heights to ride the lift with him. The siren to whom he'd secretly sung a love song last night.

He wanted to know more, wanted to know everything about her. But he didn't even have access to her last name, per Blue Sky Resort policy. All he had of her were the scraps of information that she had chosen to share with him on the slopes. Although something told him that the conversations the two had shared on the chair lift hadn't been mere chitchat for her, either. Swallowing, he struggled to maintain a casual facade.

"She specifically requested you, presumably because she had you for group." Eric looked up at the clock on the office wall. "She'll meet you by the blue flag in five—you know the drill."

James nodded, then took his leave of Eric. Dodging the group of children another instructor was leading like ducklings to the daycare center, he found Drew loitering in the hallway. "Drew."

His roommate looked up from his phone. "Hey, man! How was the bar last night?" Drew had been asleep, worn out from a long day on the mountain, when James had finally returned, and they hadn't had time to talk this morning or during lunch, since Eric had commandeered the latter for one of his lectures on resort policy.

James did a quick calculus on how much to tell his friend, who would probably discover all in the end. "I met someone," he said, keeping his voice low.

Drew's face lit up. "Oh shit, really?"

James nodded. "She—she wants to see me again."

Drew clapped a hand on James' shoulder approvingly. "Is she local? What's her name? Do I know her?"

"No, I'm not telling you, and I doubt it," he took a deep breath, "unless you taught Level One yesterday."

Drew's eyes went wide as dinner plates as understanding dawned on him. "She's—a student?"

James nodded, grimly. "It's unethical, I know."

Drew shrugged. "I mean, honestly..."

"And it can't go anywhere, since she's just here for spring break. What am I going to do, follow her home to Boston?"

Drew laughed. "It's not like you're—Wait. She's in college? Don't you think that's a little young for you?"

James sighed. "You can be in college and not be a teenager. But no, she's not in college. It's just a family trip."

"How old is she, then?"

James paused as an instructor passed. "Twenty-five."

Drew grinned. "A cougar, you say."

Rolling his eyes, James retorted, "She's a year older than I am. Not ten or twenty."

"Whatever you say, man." Drew's grin faded a little. "What are you gonna do?"

James sighed again, passing a hand over his face. "I don't know, honestly. It's... inappropriate, to say the least." But how could it be, when she was the very reason his heart beat?

Drew twisted his lips thoughtfully. "What is it?"

"I don't understand the question, Drew."

"What *is* it? Between you two. Love, lust, a little light flirtation? Because you seem to be taking this even more seriously than, you know, regular you."

It certainly wasn't mere flirtation. Not after the way she'd met his eyes last night, held his gaze through the final verses of that love song, like it was him she wanted to be holding. At first, maybe, that's all it had been, but after the past few days... No, screw that. It had never been mere flirtation. He'd known, from the moment he met her eyes. As soon as he'd caught her, held her in his arms. It was...

Wrong. It was wrong, no matter how right it—she—felt.

James pushed off the wall against which he'd been leaning. "I should go. She's waiting for me."

Drew followed him to the door, protesting. "You never told me her name—"

"Forget I told you anything."

Nothing would come of it. Nothing could come of it. However hard his heart and body ached.

James shoved open the door and strode across the packed snow to the ski racks, locating his extra-long pair with ease. Now, to find Estie...

That, too, was easy. He was drawn to her, like a needle on a compass. It was pure magnetism. He needed to be near to her, his true north.

"Estie!"

She wasn't wearing her helmet, yet. It lay by her feet, by her discarded poles and skis. She turned, and time slowed. Her hair, in its long copper plait, spun out as she twisted towards him. It hadn't been braided last night—he'd seen it in all its unruly glory, and so that's how he imagined it now. Her smile was like the sun, radiant and bright, chasing away his soul's long and lonesome night.

"James! You found me." Estie beamed.

He found himself answering her smile with one of his own, his joy temporarily unshuttered. Then reality, like a cloud, passed over the sun, and his smile faded—hers, too, followed suit.

"What's wrong?"

"Nothing," he forced himself to say. "How are you feeling today?"

"A little hungover," she laughed, apologetically. "Still, I know. I slept until ten! Can we take it slow, at first?"

"Of course." They could take it slow, on the slopes. However fast he was falling for her, they could always take it slow. "Whatever you want, Estie." *Whatever you need.*

Estie hadn't intended her request to be a double entendre, and she didn't *think* James had taken it as such, but she wasn't sure. Like last night, the air between them was charged with energy, effervescent electricity. It spiked when he spoke in reply: whatever she wanted, he'd said. Well, Estie knew what she wanted. Him. But she wasn't about to spring that revelation on him, not at noon.

"Shall we head over to the little lift? Get some greens in? You can tell me all about my turns…" She batted her eyes at him, in brazen flirtation.

He swallowed and she smiled, pleased to see that she was having some effect on him. When he spoke, his voice was a little rough around the edges. "Your turns are—"

"Intense and passionate?" She teased. "I know, but I need to work on my control."

He shook his head. "Your control has come a long way. I think it's confidence, rather the lack thereof, that's holding you back. Technically speaking, I think you could handle a blue."

Estie bit her lip. "You think so?"

James nodded, gravely. "I *know* so."

She couldn't articulate how it felt, or what it meant, that he had such faith in her. So, she flashed him an apologetic smile. "Let's table that, for the time being. Maybe at the end of the day, when we've tried all the greens."

James laughed, a rare and beautiful thing. "Of the three hundred named runs on Lonely Peak, almost a quarter of them are greens. Not even you could exhaust them all in one afternoon."

Estie suppressed a grin. "Alright, then. Let's just do a few."

James dropped his skis and stepped into them. Estie followed suit. Then he gestured to the large conveyor belt that led up to the access area for the small lift. "After you."

Their sixth trip up the mountain was different from the others, and not just because they were headed for a blue, or because for once Estie hadn't nearly fallen off the lift. As they floated thirty feet off the ground, suspended from a wire, Estie tried not to think about slipping and falling. And for once it was easy. Not because she felt confident that James would catch her before she fell, although she did, but because he was giving her plenty else to think about with his present silence, which seemed strange, strained. Usually—and she smiled, bittersweetly, to think that she could even use that word, so well had she come to know him—they chatted away about everything and nothing. Some of her best memories of this trip were her rides up the lift with him.

Perhaps he was tired—or tired of her. Perhaps this private lesson had been an imposition, a miscalculation, a mistake. Estie bit her lip. "What time is it, James?"

Automatically, he pulled out his phone. "Three-thirty."

"Oh."

He replaced the device in his jacket's inner pocket. "Is something wrong?"

She should be asking him the same thing. "No, no... I guess I was just having so much fun, I forgot it would eventually come to an end."

"What would? The fun?"

She shook her head. "No. I mean, yes, but… The lesson. I forgot it would end. Time spent with you seems so…" *Limitless*. Estie braved a glance in his direction and found him watching her with a peculiar, almost pained expression. "James?"

He didn't hesitate. "Why did you hire me for this lesson?"

"I—Because you're the best teacher I've ever had." It was true, even if it wasn't the truth.

He leveled her a look. "I'm flattered, but that's not why and we both know it."

Estie glanced away, unable to meet his gaze. Her eyes fell instead upon their ungloved hands, resting less than half an inch apart on the safety bar. Screwing her courage to the sticking point, she extended her pinky the few millimeters necessary to touch his bare skin. He inhaled sharply. For a moment, it seemed as though he would reciprocate the gesture, entwine their little fingers in a minute embrace. But a cloud passed over the sun, throwing them into cool shadow, and he pulled his whole hand away, sliding it down the bar.

"We can't, Estie."

She didn't pretend to misunderstand him. "We *shouldn't*," she corrected. There was a difference. And she wasn't even sure the latter was true. In fact, she was quite confident that it was bullshit, too.

"You're my student," he protested, weakly.

Estie shook her head and repeated his earlier pronouncement. "Only on the mountain, only between the hours of nine and four. It's almost four." She braved a glance below their dangling skis. "And technically we're not *on* the mountain."

"Estie, listen to me. There's an imbalance of power. It would be inappropriate, to say the least!"

She sighed deeply, hating that it had come to this. But they had to talk about it, the elephant in the room. "If anything, James, I have power over you."

"What? No—" But his protest fell short, probably because he knew as well as she did that it was true.

"If we… do this, and the resort finds out, I won't be the one out of a job." Estie gripped the icy bar. "Which is why…" She steeled herself for rejection, for having to somehow remove herself from this situation. Really, a ski lift was not an ideal location for a conversation like this. Still, it was too late to turn back. "I'll go, if you want me to; I'll stay on the lift, ride it back down—I'll end the lesson early and leave you alone. But not because I feel put upon, or pressured, or powerless to say no. Rather, because I don't want you to feel any of those things. I'd never forgive myself if I forced you to—"

"Stop!" James' knuckles had turned white, so tight was his grip on the safety bar. "Estie, you haven't—I don't—" He took a deep breath and his eyes found hers once more. "It's not like that."

"Then what is it like, James?"

His gaze was unwavering, and a little wild. "I want you."

Her breathing hitched and suddenly they were the only two people on, or off, the mountain. "I want you, too."

"Then why are we arguing?" His confusion was adorable.

Estie laughed, and she was surprised to find that the sound was thick with unshed tears. "I don't know," she said, desperately, her emotions gone all wobbly. "I think... I think we're both a bit scared." Did he feel this, whatever this was, as strongly as she did? Was this a trick of her moods, or something more?

He nodded. "I don't want you to get hurt."

"I won't," she assured him quickly. "Not while you're watching over me." And then it was her turn to murmur, "I don't want to hurt you."

Taking her right hand in his, weaving their fingers together, he whispered, "You won't." Then, any audience below or behind them be damned, he pressed her cold knuckles to his lips.

They held hands all the rest of the ride, until it came time to disembark. Estie managed to glide down the little hill without falling once, coming to a slow halt beside James.

"Shall we?" He asked, gesturing down the mountain.

Estie nodded and they were off.

Fifteen minutes later, give or take a few stops during which James corrected Estie's form or complimented her on her substantial improvement—all thanks to him, she reminded him, and was rewarded by a quirk of his lips and his faint blush—they arrived at the base of the mountain.

"You did it!" He smiled at her, a wide and generous curve of his lips. "You skied a blue!"

Estie forgot herself momentarily and did a little dance, earning her a chuckle from James. Gazing up at him, into those eyes of his—leaf-green and full of a longing that set her alight—she sighed and said, sincerely, "I couldn't have done it without you."

He shook his head without severing their shared gaze. "That was all you, baby."

Estie's lips parted at the endearment, which surprised her—but what surprised her more was how sweet it sounded on his lips, how right it felt, sending frissons of hot and heady feeling from her freezing toes to her fingertips.

James froze, realizing what he'd said. Quickly, he continued, "Do you want to go again? The lesson ends in ten, so we'd have to go over, but I wouldn't mind."

Estie shook her head, living for the fact that he'd slipped up and said something so sweet… and yet his words were not without a certain sensuality. "It's kind of you to offer—"

"There's nothing kind about it," James murmured, with a rare grin that was resigned to wickedness, his embarrassment forgotten. "It's selfish, really. I just want to spend time with you."

Estie felt a flush creep into her cheeks and, throughout her body, that familiar heat. "In that case, I have a proposition for you…" Leaning on one pole, Estie allowed herself to sway a little closer to James, who shuffled a step toward her, despite their being in full view of the village. "Will you be my date to the après-ski tomorrow?"

He slanted one dark eyebrow. "I wasn't aware dates were desirable at après events."

As though he could ever be anything but desirable. "Is that a no?" She felt… worse than crestfallen. Like the sun had fallen from the sky, casting the two of them into shadowy oblivion.

"No, not at all." He paused, as if he were uncertain of himself. Several skiers passed, one of them waving to James. He ignored the man, who disappeared into the line for the big lift, and then quietly, almost gravely, continued, "I'd like to be your après-ski date. Very much."

Relief flooded Estie. "Oh, thank god. I mean, good!" His broad smile shattered his serious mien, and Estie felt the heat within her rise even further. She blathered on, a little afraid of the intensity of her feelings for James. "And I promise I'm not just asking you because it's on the other side of the mountain and I don't think I can get there, much less back, without you. I'm not using you, I swear!"

He let out a little huff of laughter, a puff of white air. "Better me than ski patrol," he murmured, but Estie was too caught up in the warmth of his stare to register his words, so she just nodded.

"Can you get the afternoon off?"

"For you, I can do anything."

Estie batted at his arm playfully. But there was nothing playful about his words, or the way he said them. "Meet me here, at one?"

James nodded.

"And I should warn you—there will be drinking. But there probably won't be drugs."

James laughed, leaning back to pop out of his skis. As he gathered them in a fireman's grip, he returned, "This ain't my first après, baby."

CHAPTER 6
THE APRÈS

"WHAT TIME DO the ski lifts shut down, again?"

"Four-thirty," James supplied, shuffling his skis as they waited in line. It was a little after one, now.

"And you're sure this pass will get me to the other side of the mountain?"

He turned in time so see Estie nibble her lower lip. If they hadn't been in full view of the ski school, not to mention hundreds of resort guests, James would have swept her into his arms and taken that worried lip between his own teeth, distracting her from her racing thoughts with all-consuming kisses. Then again, they were both wearing helmets, so that strategy might not satisfy either of them. James would have to soothe Estie's frazzled nerves some other way.

He switched his poles to his right hand and wove their free fingers together. She glanced up at him, nervously.

"Should we be—"

"No one can see. And yes, this pass will get you anywhere on Lonely Peak, except the peak."

Estie frowned. "I'd need to take the tram up the ridge to get there, right?"

"Yes, and you're not going to do that." He thought of Estie, flying down a chute, and shuddered. "It's too dangerous."

"My siblings can do it," she grumbled.

James couldn't help but smile. "Oh, so *now* you want to learn to ski."

Her jaw dropped. "Who said I didn't want to learn to ski?"

He grinned at her as they shuffled forward in line, feeling uncharacteristically playful and joyously free. "I know you were only taking those lessons for me."

She swatted at him, nearly dropping her poles in the process. "You're starting to sound like Freddy."

"Oh?" He'd only met her brother once, but somehow he didn't strike James as simpatico.

Estie glared at the ground, shaking her head. "He saw right through me, when I came downstairs Tuesday morning. Said I was only signing up for a second day because I wanted to sleep with my instructor."

James cocked his head curiously, feeling the heat rise in his cheeks. "And?"

"And what?"

They were approaching the lift. James lowered his voice. "Do you want to sleep with me?"

Estie laughed, the sound like quicksilver. "You know I do."

James felt himself grinning like an idiot as they took their seats on the six-person lift. Estie did brilliantly, despite her history with chair lifts, settling in beside him with remarkable ease. They took off. "Have you lost your fear of lifts?"

"What? No, god no." She shook her head as the safety bar lowered across their laps. When it was securely in place, she clutched her poles in one hand and patted his thigh with the other. "I just know you'll never let me fall, or otherwise make a fool of myself."

He placed his hand atop hers, curling his gloved fingers around hers, and squeezed. "You're safe with me." He would never let anything happen to her, as long as he was with her. However long that happened to be.

Two chair lifts, one blue run, and two short greens later, James and Estie found themselves traversing across a trail that led to a large cabin with an overpopulated deck-turned-dance-floor. EDM pounded out from the open windows and door.

Estie turned to James, a nervous expression on her face. "That's it, I think. We followed my sister's directions exactly."

James nodded. "I've skied past this place before. Never stopped in, though."

"I can see why…" Estie muttered, ominously.

James shook his head. "Estie, I don't mind when the people around me are drinking. Or using. I wouldn't take gigs in bars if I did."

She glanced over at him, slipping a little down the slope as she did.

"Watch those edges," he warned her.

Estie huffed a laugh as she tilted her skis perpendicular to the slope and dug into the snow. "Yes, *instructor*."

"Nope." They trekked onwards, approaching the door. "Don't."

"What?" She sounded surprised. "You don't find the circumstances even a little bit sexy?"

He sighed, hating to burst what was clearly becoming her bubble. "No."

"Oh." Estie slid to a halt before the open door, and started to step out of her skis. Raising her voice above the music, she announced, "Well, I do. But we can discuss erotic role-play later, *sir*." She turned back to him with a wink, and James struggled to maintain his stern expression. "Come on, strip down! We've got an après to attend."

Estie pulled off her helmet and shook out her hair, which was, in a surprisingly cute but certainly very sweaty way, plastered to her head. James kicked off his skis, gathered hers up with his and leaned them against a nearby rack, and followed suit. "We can leave our gear out here," he started to say. "There's virtually no theft on the mountain —what?"

She pouted at him. "It's not fair!"

"What's not?"

"Your hair! You look like you walked out of a L'Oreal ad."

He smiled, smoothing his hair self-consciously. "I use a local brand, actually. It's more sustainable."

Estie rolled her eyes affectionately. "God, you're perfect. Too perfect." She extended her hand, and he took it without question. "Come on, let's see if you can dance, too."

James blanched. "You never said I'd have to dance..."

Estie laughed loudly, her earlier anxiety apparently forgotten, pulling him into the packed cabin. The lights were low and the music was loud. They found Estie's siblings fairly quickly, for all the crowd. Florence—Flo, rather—was sitting in her fiancé's lap, sipping from a flask. Freddy and—Ben, was it?—were way out in the middle of the dance floor, but they waved when they caught sight of Estie and James.

Miles smiled as they approached, shifting Flo on his lap. "You made it!"

"I'm impressed." Flo raised her eyebrows in surprise and approval.

"You should be," James countered, remembering Estie's nerves and feeling a little frustrated with Estie's siblings for so clearly dragging her outside of her comfort zone. At the same time, his chest swelled with pride; Estie had surpassed herself, skiing here today.

Estie slipped her hand through James' arm, tugging him closer. "I couldn't have done it without James—you remember James, don't you, Flo?"

Flo nodded, her wide eyes bouncing back and forth between them. James waited for her disapproval, but it never came. Instead, she seemed pleasantly amused. "How could I forget such a voice? Like listening to James Taylor himself." James thanked her for the compliment, but she waved him away. "Estie, are you drinking today?"

Estie shook her head. "No, I don't think I could ski after a drink or two. And we can't stay out here all night."

"True. Well, I think they have non-alcoholic stuff, by the bar. Go, get a drink. James looks especially thirsty." Flo grinned as she said this, clearly enjoying whatever was in that flask, and the innuendo was not lost on James.

Or Estie, apparently. She blushed, and he was reminded of the sunrise, suffusing the icy slopes. Except there was nothing cold about Estie. She was all warmth and wonder, all heat and humor. James wanted to smile whenever he saw her.

She smiled back at him, a little shyly. "Shall we?"

His brow furrowed in confusion. What was the question?

"Shall we make our way to the bar?" She clarified, her smile growing in the face of his blatant confusion. "Maybe they have mocktails!"

"I doubt it," he replied honestly, "but let's see."

They wound their way through the crowd, waited in line for a few minutes, and were rewarded for their efforts with hot chocolate—without the offered dollop of vanilla vodka.

Estie lit up as she took her first sip. "This is delicious!"

James watched, his own drink forgotten, as her tongue darted out to lick her pretty pink lips.

She caught him watching and boldly held his gaze—James found it impossible to look away. "Do you want a taste?"

Scarcely aware of what she was asking, so utterly bewildered was he by her beauty, James nodded.

"Come here," she beckoned with one crooked finger.

James stepped toward her.

"Closer, James," she whispered with wicked glee.

He did as he was told, coming to stand in her space. The toes of their boots knocked together, but neither cared.

Estie raised her free hand, hooking her fingers around the nape of his neck. Her touch was electric, and James felt his body light up in response. He shivered. Gently, Estie guided him down till their eyes were level and their mouths—

Estie captured his lips in a kiss that could have created a whole new universe. James' free hand automatically looped around her waist, drawing her flush against his chest. Hot chocolate from their cups splashed on the wooden floor but James didn't care, he didn't give a damn about anything anymore. Except Estie, and her hot, chocolatey kiss.

Someone whooped loudly and Estie pulled away. Reluctantly, James opened his eyes and let reality resume. Estie's annoying little brother and his polite boyfriend, who probably deserved better, were pointing at them and clapping. James glanced in the other direction, to find Flo and Miles cackling, also clapping. Soon enough, the whole room was applauding, watching them with wide smiles. There were a couple of drunken hoots and someone cheered.

"Do it again!" A stranger cried.

"Kiss!" Came another command. Soon enough, it turned into a chant. The cabin shook with the force of the inebriated skiers' demands. Instinctively, James tried to shield Estie with his body. But there was only so much he could do in a crowd, and being this close to her distracted him, made him want to do more than just shield her. Although, if he were being honest, he'd had more on his mind for some time.

Estie tugged on his shoulder, pulling him down to murmur in his ear. "Do you want to get out of here?"

The sunlight was blinding, after the cabin's dark atmosphere. They tramped through the bright snow, laughing and kissing and clutching each other close, making it as far as the nearest thicket of pines before tripping over their too-big boots and falling headlong into a snowdrift.

"Oof." Estie felt the breath leave her body. James rolled off of her, apologizing profusely. And then he pulled her on top of him, parting her legs so she straddled him, and she lost her breath again for a completely different reason.

Estie grinned down at James as she adjusted herself against him, aligning his hardening length against her aching core. "Is that all for me?"

James' eyes rolled back as she rolled her hips forward. When he met her gaze again, he muttered to himself as much as to her, "Fuck, yes." Then he pulled her down into a desperate kiss. All doubt, all uncertainty, all anxiety disappeared as he plundered her open mouth.

After a minute—or maybe an hour, who knew!—Estie pulled away, panting. "Can we do this?"

One of his hands was on her hip, holding her to him. The other was pulling lightly on her plait. "What?" His moss green eyes were clouded with lust and confusion.

"I mean," and Estie realized she was about to babble, but there was no stopping her once she got started, "First of all, do you want to do this? And by 'do this' I mean 'have sex with me in a snowbank on the side of the mountain that is technically your place of work?'"

He gazed at her, something akin to awe in his expression.

"And, if you do want to, which, well, I really hope you want to because I do, too—*can* we do this? Like, is it legal?"

James snorted. "No, it's definitely not legal."

Estie bit her lip, which was tender where he'd taken it between his teeth. "Okay… Does that mean we shouldn't? Do it?"

James tugged her flush against his chest. Holding her gaze, he answered her in his calm, confident way, "No."

She cocked her head. It was her turn to be confused. "What?"

"No," he repeated, a small smile flickering at the corner of his eminently kissable lips, "We should *definitely* do this." And then they were kissing again and fireworks were exploding against the closed lids of Estie's eyes.

Estie moaned, planting her hands in the snow on either side of James' head for better leverage. It was freezing, and her fingers would hurt later, but she didn't actually care. She ground against him, relishing his groans, his little gasps, the final nails in the coffin of his stoicism. Giggling against his lips, she asked in a giddy whisper, "You like that?"

He nodded, his fingers digging into her hips. "I'd like it more if you were wearing less."

"Mmm, speaking of which…" She nipped at his lower lip and he rewarded her with a ravenous kiss. "Can you get me out of these fucking boots?" They were literally dragging her down, their weight an unnecessary burden, a reminder of the reality that waited beyond the border of the dense thicket.

James laughed, lightly. "As you wish." And then he lifted her off of him and set her down beside him so that he could kneel at her feet and unbuckle her bulky boots. Gently, he eased her feet out of the claustro-phobic contraptions. Sighing, Estie wiggled her toes as James set to work on his own.

"It's a good thing it's so hot today," she remarked, her eyes on the icicle that dripped from a nearby branch.

"It's terrible," James replied, setting his boots aside. "The snow's turned to slush."

Estie shook her head, smiling. "No, I mean, it's good for us." She unzipped her vintage snowsuit in one fell swoop. "Because if it were any colder, I couldn't do this." Her eyes on his jaw, which was starting to drop, Estie shimmied out of the suit altogether. Stripped down to her long underwear, she laid the suit down and sat on it, so the snow wouldn't melt against her when things got hot. And given the way James was gazing at her, things were about to get *very* hot. They might well leave the snowbank a puddle.

"Come here," he commanded softly, as his eyes traveled the length of her, mapping her every kink and curve.

Estie started to crawl toward him, positioning herself between his spread knees. With outstretched fingers, she reached for the fastenings of his snow pants.

"No." He caught her hand in his, his staying touch gentle.

Estie met his eye quizzically.

James smiled, that rare and special smile, the one that lit his face with inner light and made her feel like everything would be more than alright. "Let me?"

Understanding dawned. Estie nodded eagerly. She hadn't shaved in a week, hadn't even brought a razor to Montana, but somehow she doubted James would care. "Have at it," she murmured, her own smile a hungry smirk.

In one swift and clever maneuver, James rolled over onto the snow-suit-turned blanked and pulled her under him, caging her with his arms. Then he caught her lips in a starving kiss. Estie sighed as he dragged his open mouth along the line of her freckled jaw and down, giving her neck the attention she'd never known it had needed. She wanted him to suck harder, to leave a mark, but she supposed she'd always have the memory. Except that, lately, she'd begun to wonder whether memory would even be enough, when it came to James—and then that worry went away, as she succumbed to the sensation of his thumb circling her sensitive nipple through her long underwear.

"May I?" James tugged on the hem of her top.

Estie nodded, and James pulled the garment up, exposing her

midriff to the mountain air. He pushed up her simple sports bra, baring her beaded nipples. The breeze was brisk, and the snow seemed to draw the warmth from the space between their bodies. But quickly James covered her left breast with his hand, cupping her ample flesh in his palm while tweaking the little bud-like tip between his index finger and his thumb. Estie's eyes really rolled back in her head, however, when he lowered his open mouth to suck on her right tit, closing his lips over her delicate areola, drawing circles around its dark peak with his clever tongue.

Estie could feel the warmth, the wetness gathering against the gusset of her cotton panties. "James," she moaned, or maybe whispered. "I need *more*."

He chuckled, the cruel man, and began to drag his lips ever so slowly down the center of her abdomen, pressing kisses to her pale skin, cast into shadow by his torso. Those capable hands of his found the waistband of her long underwear, and she shivered as he slipped one long finger between the fabric and her bare, sensitive skin. "May I?"

Again, Estie nodded. "Please."

Smiling against the swell of her belly, just below the button, he hooked a thumb into the fabric near her hips, and tugged down. Her drenched panties stuck to the garment, sliding off with it, and James laughed but the sound was cut short by his sharp intake of breath, as her glistening cunt came into view. Hastily, he discarded the long underwear, leaving it loose around her ankles, but tight enough that her lower legs were trapped together and she had to draw her knees up and let them fall to either side, butterfly-like, to give him access to the aching heart of her.

Suddenly serious, but not in the least bit stoic, James drew one long finger up the length of her labia. The both watched with bated breath as it came away wet. Then, James parted those lips of his, and sucked the tip of his finger. He groaned, and Estie grinned.

When at last he opened his eyes again, they were bright as the sun in the sky. He gestured towards her throbbing cunt, and licked his lips. "May I?"

Squirming against the snowbank, she nodded, muttering something about how he could do anything, have anything, take anything—so long as he got on with it, damnit. And then, Estie ceased to speak, ceased to breathe. Because James was doing more than tasting her. He was devouring her.

James licked, and kissed, and sucked, and savored—and his thick mustache tickled, to Estie's delight. He stroked her with his tongue and then, later, when she was panting and pouting and praying for more, with his fingers—first one went in, then two, then three, then four—his pinky, not penetrating her pink folds but simultaneously teasing her tight hole. He worked her slowly at first, picking up speed and intensity as he went, but always gentle, always with his sweet and tender sincerity. His tongue made miracles against her clitoris, even as his touch worked wonders within her wet and flexing walls.

The first time Estie came, she smiled.

The second time Estie came, she gasped.

The third time Estie came, she cried. And squirted, because apparently she could.

The wet warmth splashed against James' lips and face, and he laughed even as he licked it up eagerly. The sound was so sweet, and the sensation so sweeping, Estie thought maybe she had died. But then as she panted, breathless, and her cunt pulsed around his withdrawing fingers, James came up for air at last and reminded her with a long, lingering kiss that they were in fact alive. And when he fell to the side, and she opened her eyes, the sudden sun confirmed it. As did the melting snow against her bare knee, when she moved over to give him some room on the snowsuit.

"I wasn't expecting that," he murmured, pulling her into a close embrace. Gently, he nipped at her earlobe.

Estie giggled, turning her face into his slightly hairy chest. "Your mustache is wet."

He passed a hand over his face, then ran it through his dark, messy locks. Estie shuddered to think about the state of her own plait. "As is my hair."

Her jaw dropped. "Did I do that?"

"Well, technically I think your—"

Estie shut him up with a kiss. Then, as she smoothed his damp mustache, she murmured, "I don't want to know the mechanics of female ejaculation, James. It's enough to know that, for a fact, it does indeed exist." A coy smile curved her lips. "What are you doing tomorrow? Other than lying back and letting me have my way with you?"

He smiled, too, against her forehead. "I don't know, but whatever I do, I'm doing it with you."

CHAPTER 7
BACKWOODS BEAUTY

"Sorry, Eric." James coughed convincingly into the phone, the morning after the après. "I'm sick. I don't think I can come in today. Or tomorrow, honestly. I—" He coughed again, trying for a little phlegm. "I wouldn't want any of the resort guests to get sick."

He could practically hear Eric frown. "Are you sure? It's a big week for tips."

"Definitely." There was no way he was working today, even if Eric's line about tips had been even remotely true. For good measure, James coughed again. It was novel, lying to a man he supposed he considered a friend. A friendly acquaintance, at the very least. His boss, besides. But he'd meant it when he'd told Estie that he'd do anything for her. And lying to get out of work was hardly murder.

Ten minutes later, dressed in a flannel shirt, worn jeans, and a light jacket, James locked the apartment and headed for the road that led into town. It was too far to walk, but there would be cars passing by and James was confident that at least one driver, likely a local, would let him hitch a ride. He'd done it other times when Drew had the car.

The late morning air was brisk but bearable, and it took less than five minutes of James' sticking his thumb out for someone to slow to a halt.

"Where you headed?" The other man was older, with a bushy

beard that was as grey as the rocks that bordered the narrow chutes at the top of the mountain.

"Town," James said, simply. Blue Sky was the only town around for a fair number of miles. "You?"

"Same. Whereabouts?" As he spoke, he reached across and opened the door to the passenger seat.

James hauled himself up into the truck. "The Brown Bear." Before they'd parted ways yesterday, he and Estie had decided to meet up at the less touristy of the two coffee shops in town today, and not just because the prices were lower.

The older man nodded approvingly. "My niece works there. Alice. If you see her, tell her her Uncle Jim wants his old snowblower back. Not like she'll need it anytime soon, given that it's starting on springtime."

James inclined his head. "Yes, sir. Will do. And thank you, for the ride."

"Not a problem." They pulled back onto the road, and Jim turned on the radio.

The Brown Bear was on the same block as the Little Couloir, both of them tucked away from the touristy high street. As he hopped out of the truck, thanking Jim again and promising to pass along his message, James glanced around for a telltale flash of copper curls. He hoped Estie had found the place okay. She'd managed to locate the bar, the other night, so he doubted she'd had trouble today. His Estie could do anything she set her mind to, James knew.

Sure enough, as he pushed open the door to the coffee shop, a tall woman with long red hair sprung up from behind a small table. "James!"

He smiled. "You made it."

Estie didn't wait for him to walk over to her; she met him halfway, and with a kiss. James felt the world fall away, as reality narrowed down to the sweet taste, the silken feel of her lips against his. "I'm not a dingbat. And I have the maps app."

James gazed into her coffee brown eyes. "Who called you a dingbat?"

She laughed softly, ducking her head. "My brother. It doesn't matter."

Frowning, James pressed a kiss to the top of Estie's head, aware that they were being incredibly public in their displays of affection, but not finding it in himself to care. "I'm not sure I like your brother."

Estie laughed again, a little louder. "Oh, ignore him. Freddy's just a bit of a prick. But he's actually quite sweet, under the surface."

James raised one eyebrow.

"Sometimes."

He lifted the other.

Estie sighed. "Oh, alright. He hasn't been sweet for some time. But regardless, I'm not sharing you with him."

"I wasn't aware that was even on the table."

Estie smirked. "If he weren't madly in love with Ben, he'd absolutely make a pass at you. I mean, who wouldn't?"

James didn't understand. "Many, many people?" He hadn't always been as lucky in love—or, rather, romance—as he currently was.

Estie rolled her eyes magnificently. "Rhetorical question, James. You're a certified hottie! You just happen to live on a mountain in the middle of nowhere."

James felt the tips of his ears flush slightly, at the compliment. It was time to change the subject. "Speaking of mountains in the middle of nowhere…"

Estie's eyes lit up. "Where are you taking me?"

He shook his head, wanting this to be a surprise. Estie seemed like the kind of person who would appreciate a good surprise. Although, she had to know that they'd be hiking, because he'd asked her to wear sturdy shoes and durable clothing. "You'll see. Have you got your coffee?"

She grabbed a paper cup from the table where she'd been sitting as she waited for him to arrive. "Do you need anything?"

You.

Her eyes flashed and her smile widened, and James realized he must have said that out loud.

"Come on, cowboy." She slipped her free hand into his, tangling their fingers. "Take me away."

❄

The trail was long and winding, and bordered by forest on either side. Once, they had to cross a creek, and James held Estie's hand as she balanced her way across a fallen branch that doubled as a bridge. The sunlight streamed, and the birds sang, and the wildflowers peeked up from melting patches of snow. As they ducked under some low hanging leaves, Estie started to laugh—not because the activity was especially amusing, but for the sheer joy she was feeling. "Where are we going?"

Smiling that special smile of his, the one he seemed to reserve just for her, James said simply, "You'll see."

"Are you about to murder me? I should warn you, I've got a good scream…"

"Then I should inform you that there's no one around for miles to hear you, should you in fact scream."

Estie narrowed her eyes at him, tripping over a stray branch in the process. He caught her, however, and held her in the circle of his arms for a long moment. Which she ruined, by asking, rather breathlessly, "Are you badly quoting *The Princess Bride* at me?"

James set her on her feet, but not before stealing a quick kiss which left her prone to more tripping and no less breathless. "I couldn't be."

It took her a moment, but eventually Estie recovered enough from the impromptu kiss to remember what they were talking about. "What do you mean?"

"I've never seen it," he said with a shrug, then started walking again, his hand reaching for hers, twining their fingers together.

But Estie didn't budge, so great was her shock, which meant it was James' turn to stumble in his stubborn refusal to relinquish her hand. She steadied him, then demanded, "How have you never seen *The Princess Bride*? Did you grow up in a cave?"

"Mmm, our only movies were the shadows on the wall."

She snorted. "Okay, Plato. But seriously, this is an egregious situation. Is there a television, wherever you're taking me? Do we have the capacity to stream cinematic classics?"

He shook his head.

Estie frowned. "We should head back to town—"

"We've been hiking for an hour, Estie. We're not turning around now. Besides, it's just past the bend, behind that snowy thicket."

She eyed him suspiciously. "What is?"

"The cabin where I'm going to murder you."

Estie sniffed. "I'd much rather you make love to me."

James grinned, reeling her in. "Oh?"

Estie inhaled the scent of him—pine needles, like a walking Maine wood. She stared up into his moss green eyes, then let her gaze fall to his lips, which he licked. "Oh," she whispered. And then she was kissing him again. Longer, this time. Her arms wrapped around him with no intention of ever letting go.

Except, James had other plans. "Trust me, Estie," he murmured, his lips against hers. "You'll want to see this view."

She pouted up at him, although the difference in their height was only a few inches. They really were both abnormally tall. "But I like this one."

He laughed, knocking their noses together. "And you'll have this one for the rest of time. Just, trust me, Estie. One more time."

His words stole her breath away, and she didn't have to wonder whether he meant them. James wasn't a flippant person. He wasn't reckless or insincere. He wouldn't promise forever and then give her just one single night. The better question was what she wanted.

Estie had told herself that this thing with James would—could—only ever be just a fling. So, what would happen if she admitted to herself that she wanted more than a fling? Would she be breaking her own heart, if she were honest with herself about wanting—needing—everything?

Before Estie could think, or feel, herself into a quandary, James led her past the thicket, around the trail's bend. Sure enough, the view was spectacular. The mountain, majestic in its loneliness. The view held a hint of melancholy, too, but Estie refused to dwell on that particular emotion. What *it* promised. Instead, she gazed out upon the work of some god, or nature herself, and let James, who was standing a step behind her, squeeze her hand. Her heartbeat filled the silence, hammering away as he nuzzled the exposed skin of her neck, brushed his lips over that sensitive stretch.

"Shall I show you the inside? It's not so impressive, but it is comfortable."

Estie turned and found herself in his embrace. "Comfortable enough for us to stay?" She was asking for the night, at least, if nothing else. But in her heart, she was hoping for eternity.

James smiled, a mischievous thing. "I've yet to test the mattress, considering the fact that this is my first time borrowing this place for an overnight—from friends, to be clear, not some internet stranger —but..."

She crashed into him, kissing him with a passion she'd never known, much less shown to another person. When she came up for air, at last, she whispered, "It'll do."

"This is what it looks like on the inside," James announced, as he unlocked the door several minutes later. He reached for Estie, who had been investigating the weathered outside of the small structure, snaking an arm around her waist and pulling her to him until they stood side by side, each gazing at the other, instead of looking in.

Estie leaned in for a more leisurely kiss. After a minute, she mumbled against his lips, "*This* is the cabin where you're going to murder me?"

He knocked his nose against hers, smiling. "I'd much rather make love to you," he whispered, an echo of her earlier words. And then he took her hand and tugged her into the cabin.

Estie glanced around, sizing up her surroundings. The cabin appeared to be comprised of one large room, furnished with a massive bed and two side tables, as well as a small breakfast table with two worn chairs before a small fireplace, and a small but serviceable kitchenette to one side. On second glance, she noticed the attached bathroom, the door open just enough for her to catch a glimpse of a porcelain tub.

"It's lovely," she said, and she meant it. The furniture was a haphazard collection of styles, but all of them were variations on the hand-carved, wooden theme. The cabin had a quaint, rustic quality to it, but it was large enough that she didn't feel in the least bit claustrophobic. Estie rather thought she could be very happy here, way out in the woods, writing all day and making love all night. "But let's skip the tour."

James, who had been watching her nervously, relaxed as soon as she signaled her approval. Now, he raised one eyebrow. "Oh? Do you have a better idea as to how we could occupy ourselves?"

Estie began to unzip her coat, slowly and without taking her eyes off of James, whose lips began to curve in an anticipatory smile. He was hungry—for her. As hungry as she was for him—and had been, ever since the après. Ever since they'd stumbled into that snowbank, where he'd set her aflame, again and again and again.

Estie had been exhausted by James' efforts, by her own, climactic reactions to his careful touch. But she hadn't been sated. She might never be sated, now that James had awoken in her this positively primal hunger.

"Well?" She began to shrug off her coat, letting it fall to the ground in a clatter of zippers. "Are you just going to stand there and watch me?"

James shook his head, then surprised Estie by sinking to one knee.

"What are you—" Her half-articulated question was answered when he set to work on the laces of her boots. In no time at all, thanks to his clever and quick fingers, she was free of the mudcaked weights. James pressed a kiss to each of her clothed kneecaps, then stood and started on his own jacket. He made quick work of that, too, as well as his own boots.

"Wait!" Estie held out a hand as he began to unbutton his worn flannel.

James frowned. "Am I moving too fast? We can slow down."

"No," Estie shook her head emphatically. "Not at all. I just… I want to undress you." She bit her lip, watching his throat work. "Is that… Can I undress you?"

James nodded, swallowing. "I'd like that. Very much."

Her socks sliding on the hardwood floor, Estie shuffled closer to

James. She slipped, slightly, and he caught her in both his arms—an echo of their first meeting. Estie smiled at the memory of that fateful day, the day that everything—her whole life, it seemed—had changed. And all because she'd met James. Well, fallen into his arms, more precisely.

James angled his head to the side and drew her in close, taking her lips in a tender kiss that nevertheless demonstrated his red-hot desire, his characteristic intensity, his rare impatience. Before he pulled back, Estie nipped at his lower lip, eliciting a groan from James as he reclaimed her mouth in another, still more starving kiss.

As she explored James' open mouth, offering him herself as sustenance, Estie spread her hands across his chest, smoothing over his soft flannel and the curving musculature it hid. She fumbled for the buttons, prying his shirt open, one fastening at a time. When she worked on the final button, which fell below the waistband of his jeans, Estie allowed her fingers to graze against the denim placket. Her pinky traced a curious trail south, and she was rewarded first by the simple fact of his hardness, like a river stone, and then by the way his cock twitched under her explorations.

Estie smiled against James' eager lips.

And then she pressed a kiss to the corner of those lips. Another, to his cheek. And then a third, to the hard edge of his exquisitely chiseled jaw. Then she dragged her open mouth down to suck on the soft, sensitive skin of his bare neck. Cupping his dick through the denim, Estie squeezed, once, drawing from James a guttural groan and a rare expletive. Smirking, she nibbled at his neck, bringing her hands back up to caress his rippling abdominals.

Estie gasped, pulling away to gaze down at James' stomach. Her eyes were drawn inevitably to the trail of dark hair that led further south, but she forced them up to count his deliciously defined muscles. "Do you have an eight pack?"

James huffed a laugh, and when Estie glanced back up she noticed that the tips of his ears were a faint pink. "I think just a six pack," he whispered, as though torn between pride and embarrassment.

"Regardless," she murmured, pressing a kiss to the curve of his collarbone. "You have a beautiful body. And face," she added, after a moment. "And mind." She shot him a mischievous glance. "But most of all, you have a beautiful mustache."

He was blushing now, the pink had traveled to his cheeks, but he didn't seem embarrassed anymore. "You don't think I should shave it?"

Estie gasped, swatting playfully at his shoulder. Then she let her hand linger there, in order to push his shirt off his shoulder and down his arm. Estie beckoned to James, who had quickly shrugged out of the shirt and was beginning to fold it. "Don't fold that shirt, James."

He looked up at her, confused. "Why not? It'll wrinkle—"

"Because if you are so lucid as to be able to fold a fucking shirt in my presence..." Estie pulled off her own shirt and let it fall to the floor in one fell swoop.

James' eyes widened as he gazed down at her full breasts, practically spilling out of her favorite bra.

"...then that means I'm not doing a good enough job of seducing you." She trailed her fingertips along his bare arms, up and over his shoulders, and let her palms settle on his pecs. She sighed happily, carding the dark hair she found there. "Besides," she added, practically purring, "don't you want to know why I think you should never shave your mustache?"

His hands found her waist and squeezed. "Tell me."

"Because I like the way it looks. And how it tickles when you kiss me... wherever you kiss me." She nudged his chin with her nose, pushing his head back so that she could suck on his bare throat. "And most of all, I like when it gets wet. Because that means you've been buried deep in my pussy, kissing and sucking and licking me."

James growled, capturing her mouth with his. He feasted on her lips like he was a dying man and she was his last meal. Like he had been stuck in the desert for days and she was the oasis he had happened upon. Like the desperate, delicious noises they both made were lyrics to their lips' song. Panting, he pulled back. "Estie, baby, can I eat you out?"

She gazed at him, drunk on pleasure and his warm embrace.

"Please?"

Estie smiled, and shook her head. "Later, James. Right now, I want you inside of me."

He nodded, once, and suddenly she was in the air, in his arms, being carried toward the massive bed. He placed her on the duvet like she was a princess, spellbound to sleep or else in search of a pea. But the only magic there, in that room, was between James and Estie. And there was no irritant, not under the mattress or anywhere else. Everything was as it should be. As for tomorrow, and what it might bring, well, Estie would think about that in the morning.

Accordingly, she set to work on the fastenings of her jeans.

CHAPTER 8
AS YOU WISH

JAMES PRACTICALLY RIPPED a hole in his jeans, in his haste to take them off. He tossed them to the floor, no longer caring where they landed or whether they would be wrinkled in the morning. He was too busy staring at Estie, who lay on the bed, wearing nothing but a bra, out of which her breasts seemed to strain, and a pair of panties, whose gusset was dark with the evidence of her desire.

She watched him from atop the duvet, her eyes daring him to do something. But James was overwhelmed by his own desire. He was helpless to it, a mere sailor in its storm.

"Come here, James," she whispered, curling her index finger.

He stepped closer to the bed, until his knees bumped against the mattress' edge.

Estie sat up, propping herself up on one hand while her other reached for him. Her slender fingers stroked a line from his aching balls to the tip of his dick, which was straining against the waistband of his faded blue boxers.

"What have we here?" She asked, playfully, knowing full well the answer. Estie hooked a finger into the waistband of his boxers and swiftly tugged them down, allowing James' cock to spring free and heavy. "Oh my," she murmured, glancing up at him. She licked her lower lip, then took it between her teeth. "So long and thick, and ever so hard... Is this all because of me?"

James nodded, scarcely able to speak.

Estie smiled like a cat that had got the cream. She swiped the pad of her finger across the tip of his dick. James hissed in pleasure, and with the pain that was restraint. Her fingertip came away wet, covered in pearly precum. Promptly, Estie opened her mouth and, earning herself a garbled moan from James, sucked the substance from her finger. "Delicious," she whispered, almost to herself. "May I?" She gestured to his dick.

James nodded, managing a strained, "As you wish."

Estie came up on her knees and crawled toward the edge of the bed. She licked her palm then took him gently in hand, stroking and squeezing him with warm, wet fingers. James bit his lip, hard. Then, Estie lowered her head and pressed a kiss to his damp tip.

James muttered an expletive.

Estie kissed him again, lingering this time, then her tongue darted out to lap up the precum that was spilling from the head of his cock. Then she opened her mouth and sucked him long and hard. She hummed with her own pleasure and the vibrations sent shivers up and down James' body, until his legs nearly gave out from the beauty of it all—of Estie, most of all. Because she was always gorgeous, but she was especially beautiful when she looked up at him, her brown eyes wide and bright, her pretty pink lips stretched around his dick.

Swallowing once more, she drew back and let his cock fall from her lips—catching it gently in her hand. Estie gazed up at him, her eyes dark with hunger. "I want more," she murmured, reaching up to draw him down. "I want you, inside of me. And I don't mean orally."

James nodded, pressing a quick kiss to her lips. Then he reached for his jeans, into their back pocket, and pulled out a strip of three condoms.

Estie laughed, catching ahold of his wrist and tugging him onto the bed, so that he was on top of her, caging her beautiful—but not nearly bare enough for their purposes—body. "Let me guess," she said, the corners of her eyes crinkling, "safety first?"

Chuckling, James tore open one of the packets. "You know me."

Estie nodded, with a strange solemnity. "I do."

James shivered as he rolled on the condom, and not just with pleasure, or because the lubricated latex was cool against his sensitive cock. "Are you ready?"

Estie had unhooked her bra, freeing her breasts. James gazed at them with open admiration, his hand coming up to tweak her hard nipple, like an unripe raspberry. Estie arched into his tender touch, and he cupped first one breast, then both, massaging them gently and tracing swirling patterns around her areolae. "Just let me take off my—"

But James got there first, hooking his fingers into her pink cotton panties and practically tearing them off in his haste to be united with her, to be inside of her. He tossed them to the floor. Then he licked his fingers and began to stroke her labia; her dark pink folds, whose curves and quirks he planned to memorize, were already soaking wet.

"May I?" He extended a single finger, probing at her entrance.

Estie nodded, her eyes fluttering closed and her lips forming a soft curve.

James entered Estie gently, easing his way into her tight cunt with just his index finger. She was hot and wet and ready for him. Gradually, he pushed a second finger inside of her, stretching her ever so slightly. He curled his fingers north, running them along the ceiling of her cunt, where she was softer and more sensitive.

Estie moaned. "James, please!"

"Do you want more of this?" He murmured, lengthening his strokes. "Or do you want my cock?"

"I want your cock," she gasped. The words rushed out of her. "I want your hard cock in my pussy. Can't you feel how wet I am for you, James? I want you. I *need* you." She whined as he altered the angle of his ministrations. "Fuck me, please?"

James nodded, but Estie's eyes were still closed. "Yes," he managed, his voice rough with arousal. Then he spread her legs, nudging her knees far to either side of him, and guided his cock to her entrance. He let it rest there, twitching slightly as he felt her wet warmth, the promise of what was to come. Then he pushed forward, entering her slowly.

James' eyes rolled back into his head as pleasure flooded his core.

She felt like velvet, like silk, like satin. And she was hot and tight, wetter than fucking water.

Estie's moan cut off into a whimper as he bottomed out.

Cupping her breast with one hand, propping himself up over her with the other, James gave Estie a moment to adjust to his length, then snapped his hips.

"Fuck!" Estie arched up, her eyes opening wide as he started to pump, twisting his hips. "Yes, James! Give it to me."

James felt wild and free, desirable and desiring. After a moment, with a nod of encouragement from Estie, he flipped her over onto her stomach then pulled her up onto her hands and knees. James reentered her carefully.

Immediately, doubtless due to the new angle, Estie let out a long, languid moan. "Fuck me, James. Harder!"

James pumped into her, even as she steadied herself on one hand and reached down with the other to stroke herself. "Yes," he groaned. He wanted her to find her pleasure, to come around his cock. James put a hand on the headboard to steady himself, gripping the wood with white knuckles. His vision was beginning to blur, and he no longer felt quite tethered to this earth. "I think I'm going to—"

But then Estie let out a desperate whimper and her cunt began to flutter and flex around his swollen length.

Her orgasm was the final straw for him. James thrust hard, bottoming out, and held. He saw stars as he emptied himself inside the condom, inside the woman for whom, he was now certain, he had been made. Without Estie, there would be no James. Now, always.

Estie trailed a lone finger down James' chest and over the raised ridges of his abdominals, where a dark trail of hair led down to a cock that still twitched, from time to time, even after James had spent himself inside of her. As she traversed his musculature, like a mogul skier in slow motion, she hummed an old James Taylor tune.

"I can play that one, you know."

She lifted her head from James' shoulder to look him in the eye. "Really?" She wasn't, she supposed, surprised.

He nodded, pressing a kiss to her forehead. Estie was sure it was still a bit damp with sweat, but James didn't seem to mind. It was his doing, besides. He'd really put her through her paces. "If I had my guitar with me right now, I'd prove it to you."

Estie laughed, tucking herself back in under his chin. "I believe you. But I do still want to hear it." She smiled at the memory of his secret serenade, that night at the Little Couloir. "You have the voice of an angel."

She felt the tremor of his faint laughter. "And you believe in angels?"

Estie shook her head. "Not really. Not until I met you." She snuggled closer to him. "My guardian angel, always catching me before I fall."

"Always," he murmured into her hair, before smoothing it back beneath his chin.

"Is my hair in your face?" She asked, with amusement. "Is it getting caught in your extremely sexy, vaguely seventies mustache?" Estie knew her hair must be a mess. It always was, after sex.

She felt James nod, his jaw tapping against the top of her head. He never lied, but his honesty was without judgment. "I don't mind."

Estie closed her eyes. "Good, because I didn't bring a brush." Then she opened them again, in alarm. "Oh god. I didn't bring a brush! Or a toothbrush!" Estie started to sit up.

James, however, pulled her back down again until she was flush against his warm chest. "There's a brush in the bathroom," he murmured, sounding distinctly as though his eyes were closed. "Although we might have to share the spare toothbrush."

Ordinarily, Estie would not have liked the idea of sharing a toothbrush with a man she was—well, whatever it was she and James were doing together. Having sex, as of five minutes ago. But this was James. He made her feel safe and comfortable. He didn't judge her for being human, for having psychological needs or biological functions. And, what's more, she didn't judge him. "Well, then," she whispered at last, carding her fingers through his chest hair. "I suppose that's alright."

He nodded again, settling deeper into the pile of down pillows. "What about god?"

"Are we to share him, too?"

James chuckled at her little joke. "No, I meant… Do you believe in god? Any god, or gods, at all?"

Estie shrugged. "Not really. I was raised Episcopalian, but by that I just mean I went to Sunday school for a few years, from when I was in kindergarten until maybe fourth grade."

"Why did you stop?"

Estie smirked. "I caused a minor scandal." She tilted her head up in time to see James' eyebrows rise.

His voice was an amused rumble. "Do tell."

"Do you remember in *Love Actually* when they kiss during 'All I Want For Christmas Is You?' And the curtain comes up on them, still kissing?" Estie smiled to remember the looks on the parishioners faces at her own theatrical debut. "Something like that, only I was supposed to be playing a shepherd and I made one of the Wise Men miss his cue. The nun who was in charge of the whole thing went looking for us when she noticed that, of the three Magi, only two had managed to arrive in Bethlehem for the birth."

James laughed, smoothing his palm absently along her bare arm. "I thought the Wise Men arrived after the birth."

"It's a church pageant, James. They have to condense the timeline a bit." She shook her head, smiling. "What about you? Are you religious? You clearly know your Jesus origin story."

James shook his head firmly. "No, that's just intellectual curiosity. But a lot of us are. I think the structure of religion, and the community you sometimes find, can help people to avoid relapse. And, depending upon your denomination, there's that promise of forgiveness. Which is quite something. But I prefer to seek solace in the open skies, to find my peace out on the water and on mountainsides. For me, and this isn't true of all ski instructors, not even remotely, but for me, my life is about discipline. And maintaining my wellbeing, not just my sobriety. This lifestyle requires me to take care of myself. Simply put, safety first —and the responsibility I have to others, to my employers, to my coworkers, and to my students, especially—means I can't use."

Estie propped herself up on one elbow to stare at James in something akin to awe.

He frowned, sitting up with his back against the headrest. "What's that look for?"

"Nothing," she said, joining him. "You just aren't usually so loquacious. I liked what you had to say, by the way," she added, when he looked sideways at her, uncertain. "I'm—You're really something, you know that? I admire you."

The tips of his ears turned faintly pink. "Likewise," he murmured.

"So," Estie said, taking a deep breath. "It's the seasonal life for you?"

James nodded. "What about you, do you think you could ever uproot yourself, the way I do?"

To her own surprise, Estie found herself nodding right back at him. "I do, actually. Especially since coming out here—to Montana, I mean —and spending time away from my family." Estie ignored the urge to add, *with you.* "I've always wanted to travel, to see the world outside of my neighborhood. And I think it could really help me to master the rhythm of my moods, if I were more in touch with the changing of the seasons." She bit her lip. "But I wouldn't describe it as uprooting myself."

"No?"

"It's like trees or mushrooms, isn't it? They have lots of roots, going in lots of directions, extending far beyond the shadows of their caps or canopies. And mushrooms, I think—but you tell me—can sprout up anywhere within that network. Sometimes really far from where they started. But I don't know." Estie yawned even as she shrugged. "Most of what I know about mushrooms I learned from a Shirley Jackson novel."

James' expression was quizzical, at first, but quickly turned concerned. "You're tired."

Estie shook her head, fighting off another yawn. "No, I'm just—It's late." Then she grinned up at him. "And we really did put this bedframe to the test."

He smiled, his hands coming to cradle her cheeks before his lips found hers for a long and lingering kiss. As they broke apart, James lifted the duvet. "Shall we?"

Estie sighed. "Oh, alright. But one more question. You mentioned the water? What is it you do in the off-season?"

"There is no off-season, for me. In the summer I teach sailing on a small island in Maine."

"What isla—" But Estie cut herself off with another, enormous yawn. Grumbling beneath her breath, she slipped under the duvet cover.

James, who was now yawning, too, nevertheless managed a fond smile beneath his thick mustache as he joined her in the duvet's cocoon. "I'll tell you tomorrow, Estie."

She snuggled up beside him. Her eyelids fluttered closed despite her attempts to keep them open. "You promise?"

Rubbing the tip of his nose against hers, he nodded. "I'm not going anywhere."

"Good morning, starshine," a familiar tenor crooned in her ear.

Estie smiled into James' chest, her cheek pressed against its slight peppering of hair. "The earth says hello," she mumbled in answer.

James laughed, loud enough to wake her properly, and Estie blinked up at him blearily. "I didn't think you'd get that reference," he said at last, gazing down at her with his bright green eyes.

"And I didn't think you laughed or smiled this much." Estie snuggled closer into his embrace, letting her eyelids flutter closed again. "You seemed so serious, in class."

"I *am* serious," James protested, slightly sorrowfully. "Drew says I take everything, including myself, too seriously. But not you."

Estie opened her eyes at that, cocking one eyebrow. "You don't take me seriously?"

James leveled her with a look. "I take you more seriously than I've ever taken anything or anyone in my life. Myself included. What I meant was, with you, I feel free. To smile, to laugh, to breathe."

Estie, on the other hand, found herself struggling to breathe after

James' declaration. What the hell was she supposed to say to *that*? "James, I—" He waited for her to finish her thought, but Estie *hadn't* thought. She'd just—It didn't matter, in the bright light of the morning after. It wasn't possible, what she wanted from him and from herself. Reality came over her like a crash of ice water, as cold as the frost on the windowpanes. "I've got a plane to catch."

She sat up, twisting to the side, and in doing so nearly missed the mournful look that flashed across James' face before it was replaced by the same old stern and somber mien that meant nothing, and everything.

Estie rubbed the sleep from her eyes with slightly more vigor than the task required. "What time is it?"

"Eight, and there's a cup of coffee waiting for you. I think I managed a decent brew."

Estie paused, confused. "You don't know how to make coffee?"

James shrugged, sitting up even as she swung her legs over the edge of the bed. "I haven't made a pot in years, not since I got clean..." But his voice seemed to fade, and Estie realized, belatedly, what a picture she must have made: naked and unashamed, the morning sun and his gaze warming her freckled skin as she strode in the direction of the cabin's little kitchen.

"Oh, come on," she said, coquettishly and against her better judgment. But she couldn't help the brief, erotic indulgence. "You've seen me naked before."

James blushed, the tips of his ears lighting up in a pink flush. "Twice," he stated, without blinking. "In the snowbank, and under the sheets."

"And that's not enough?" Estie asked, although she knew his answer. She also knew they were playing with fire, having this conversation hours before she was supposed to get on an airplane and fly— far, far away. Swallowing, and tearing her eyes from his face, she changed conversational tacks. "Is there anything to eat? Or should I forage, alfresco?" She gestured to her naked body in an attempt at lightening the mood, which had taken another turn for the morose. Or maybe that was just Estie, being maudlin.

She didn't actually know what this—what she—meant to him. And she wasn't about to ask. That would be throwing caution to the wind. Which she'd already done, more than enough—with her words as well as her actions. And it would be worse this time, worse than the whole week's recklessness combined—more dangerous than a manic episode, deadlier than depression's throes.

Estie had seized the day, seized the week. But it would have been better for both of them if James had left while she was still asleep. Not that he was the kind of man who would—never mind.

A shiver crept up Estie's exposed spine, and she found herself suppressing a full-body shudder. But it was just a draft, or overzealous AC. Estie glanced around as she stepped into the kitchenette. A draft, she reckoned, again, as this cabin didn't have air conditioning.

A ceramic mug, looking decidedly hand-crafted—there was a studio in town, she'd passed it on the way to the trail—waited for her on the off-white counter. Estie wondered, briefly, before she shut the thought down, whether James had made it himself. She could just see him, on one of his rare days off: his muscular thighs spread wide, a throwing wheel between his knees, his face furrowed with focus, and that fire of his lighting those deep, dark eyes—but that wasn't an image she needed to imagine.

The mug, sporting a slightly lopsided handle, was filled to an inch below the brim with steaming liquid—such a rich, dark brown, it might as well have been black. A black hole, to swallow her, whole.

Estie shook herself. Coffee! Strangely, it didn't seem all that appetizing, this morning. Except that James had made it for her, despite not having made coffee in years. He'd done his best, for her, so she'd do her best, for him—to drink it and say nothing.

Say nothing of the storm that was brewing inside her. The battle between her head and her heart. Between logic and I—well, feeling. Her therapist would tell her to find balance between the two, but there was no middle path, not this time. There was only reality and ruin. The facts and her feelings.

Christ, Estie needed to call her therapist. And take her meds! If only because the routine would soothe her—it was only eight; she wasn't running late.

Estie pinned a careful smile on her face before turning away from the counter. Bright, but not sunlike. Cheery, chipper. Polite. "Is there milk?"

James shook his head, frowning. "I'm afraid not. My friends don't use the cabin often enough to justify keeping fresh—"

"Got it. I understand. It's fine!" Estie stretched that smile a little wider, even as her cheeks felt tighter. And her heart, heavier. "I can rough it, a bit. I may be a delicate flower, but..."

"You're not a delicate flower, Estie. You're a centaurea Montana."

Estie nearly spat out her coffee, and not just because it tasted as bitter as she felt. "I'm a centaur?" That was... fanciful, for a man who didn't exactly indulge in fancies. But that was it, wasn't it? She didn't know him that well!

Estie turned her attention to James, who was shaking his head, and ignored the voice inside her head—no, surely that was her heart, her treacherous, untrustworthy heart—that said she knew him better than she'd known her last two boyfriends, combined. And each of those relationships had lasted months, not days.

"Not a centaur, Esther. Centaurea Montana. Also known as the mountain cornflower, or the mountain bluet. It's a perennial, and ever-green. It grows in gardens and valleys and high on mountainsides, all across North America and Europe. Wherever its seeds land, it finds a way to survive, to grow. To thrive. It's strong and it acclimates. It's resilient, persistent, brave. *You* are resilient, persistent, and brave." He took her wrist as he searched her eyes, waiting for permission to reel her in once more.

Estie found herself breathless, again. James spoke with such intensity, and she knew he meant every word of what he said. He didn't lie, or exaggerate. He wasn't fickle or afraid. Which was why...

Estie stumbled back, her wrist slipping out of his slackening grip. "I—I have to catch a plane, James." She could see and feel the fire in his green eyes fade, until they were as cool as moss growing in a sapling's shade. Estie felt like a monster, giving him nothing, a repetitive non-sequitur for an answer. But he was wrong. She might be resilient, but she wasn't brave. Not brave enough to stay, to throw the rest of her life away.

James nodded, slowly. He wasn't going to fight her on this, was he?

Estie felt a pang of pain, but understood that fundamentally it was her responsibility to choose to stay. She couldn't blame him for not fighting for her, when she had so clearly communicated her desire to leave.

"We'll make this work, Estie." She wished she could believe him, the way he seemed to believe himself. "I promise. I'll give you my number, so you can just… Call me, when you land. Okay?"

CHAPTER 9
ON A JETPLANE

ESTIE TURNED up the volume on her headphones and stifled a sob.

Meanwhile, Stevie Nicks crooned about mountains, love, and self-destruction. Estie knew about all three, all too well.

She stared at the dead screen ahead of her, blinking back the blur. Swallowing hard, she gave a furtive glance to her left, away from the closed window into which she was cuddled, as though the uncomfortable curve of the airplane cabin could protect her from the onslaught of emotion inside.

The woman in the seat next to her was shushing a red-faced baby, and in the aisle seat a man was reading a magazine. No one seemed to be aware that she was on the verge of breaking down. Fortunately, her family were scattered in seats all along the plane's length, so none of them would see or hear her cry. Some of them would have known why, and that... Well, Estie would have been mortified to see the pity in their wide brown eyes.

Estie pulled out her phone and paused the song, but left the headphones in her ears, to dull the bustling sounds of the cabin mid-flight. She didn't need some mirror in the sky to tell her what love was. *This* was love—messy, not meticulous. Utterly unplanned. There was a burning, tugging, tearing sensation in her heart. As though she'd been cleaved to James, over the course of the past few days, and now, now that she dared to drag herself away from him, she was being cleaved in two.

There was the part of her that had to go, had to return to reality—because she had responsibilities, whatever those were, and a ticket for a window seat on a Boston-bound plane.

And then there was the part of her that had remained, would always remain, for the rest of her days, on a mountainside in Blue Sky, in a cozy cabin with James.

The baby to her left began to wail. The mother grimaced at Estie, apologetically. Estie grimaced back in acceptance and understanding and unrelated agony. Then she turned her face into the curve of the cabin, into the window that was closed so the baby could sleep, but really so that Estie didn't have to see the mountains and the valleys, the wide open spaces where she'd felt loved and free, all of it fading into the distance as the plane gained altitude, and Estie lost—everything.

Well, not everything. She still had her phone, with his number like a hidden treasure. Estie pressed the rectangular glass screen to her sternum and tried to breathe. Her hands, clutching the phone, were cold—her circulation had always been a bit questionable. Now, tears leaked from her tightly shut eyes, warming them with their wet heat. Another sob, this one less successfully stifled.

"Are you alright?"

Estie almost didn't hear her neighbor's inquiry, between the noise-cancelling headphones and the desperate drumbeat of her dying heart. She sniffled, wiping her eyes against her fisted knuckles. Then Estie turned, a fraction of an inch, to face the new mother. "Sorry?"

"Are you alright?" The woman frowned. "I don't mean to intrude, I just... Do you need to talk about it?"

What was there to talk about? Estie had left behind the potential love of her life. Sure, she had his number, and could text him on occasion. But long distance had never been her forte. She was sure to fuck this up. And it wouldn't be fair to James, to keep him in however many hundred-mile chains. Not when he was so full of life, so good and giving, expecting so little in return. He deserved better than what she could give him: a half-life, lived between phone screens.

Soon enough, their yet-unspoken love would wither, like a cut cornflower, and die.

Except, Estie knew with prophetic certainty, that she would never forget him. Not his face, not his name, not the way he took skiing and sex and everything in between so seriously. Not his voice, full of vibrato, raised in song. Not the calluses on his fingertips from strumming his guitar. Not the feel of his hands through layers of snow gear, holding her steady, catching her mid-fall. Not the quirk of his lips, when she managed to surprise him into a smile. Not the color of his irises, like new moss among the roots of ancient trees.

The woman was waiting for an answer.

"No, thank you." Estie didn't need to talk. She needed to write. And then, as soon as they landed, she needed to call James and tell him what she'd been too scared to say, this morning and yesterday. All week, really—ever since that first, fateful day.

I love you.

And then they would figure out a way to make their relationship work. Because anything was better than this pain she was in. Anything was better than losing him. Even a half-life, lived between screens.

Just then, the plane gave a jolt, followed by a shudder. Estie's phone slid into her lap, lodging between her closed thighs, as Estie gripped her armrests to steady herself.

A voice came over the speakers. "Good afternoon, ladies and gentlemen. We will be experiencing some slight turbulence. The seatbelt sign is now on. Please return to your seats immediately."

"Shoot," said the mother, who was now wrestling with the cap on a bottle of baby formula or breastmilk or something—Estie didn't know the first thing about parenting. "I can't—Damnit."

"Do you want me to try?" Estie offered, hoping to return the kindness the woman had shown her moments earlier.

"Could you? It's hard, juggling this one," she indicated the baby, "and his bottles, too."

Gingerly, Estie accepted the open bottle, full of creamy white liquid, and the cap. But as she held the bottle carefully over her lap, the plane veered suddenly to the right. Warm liquid poured like a waterfall from the open bottle, crashing down into Estie's lap—onto her phone, still lodged between her thighs.

Estie gasped. Righting the bottle, she quickly screwed on the cap, but it was too late. The damage was done. Most of the liquid had landed directly on her phone and was now pooled around the device. "Shit!"

"Oh! I'm so sorry—here, take this!" The mother was already handing Estie a clean burping cloth.

Quickly, Estie snatched up her phone, ignoring the slow trickle of the liquid as it seeped into her jeans and down, between her clamped thighs. She turned it off immediately, ignoring the way the screen was blinking, seizing, then blotted it with the cloth until it looked and felt dry. Then, tucking it into the pouch attached to the back of the seat in front of her, she turned her attention to herself.

Five minutes and a long visit to the bathroom later, Estie felt brave enough to turn the phone back on. Except that when she reached for it, and held down the power button, no apple or sliding bar appeared on the screen. It was well and truly dead. Which wouldn't be more than an inconvenience, except...

Her phone hadn't backed up since before she'd entered James' contact information. She might not—

Estie blinked back fresh tears.

She might have just lost his number, permanently. How the hell would she tell him she loved him, now? How would she make that promise, the one on the tip of her tongue, that they'd make this work, the love that lived between them?

James loitered in the center of town, watching the tourists pop in and out of shops that thrived during the colder months but struggled to survive each summer. He'd hiked back down with Estie, who'd been strangely silent the whole time, absent her usual mirth. A mood swing, she'd said. Nothing to do with anything. But James couldn't help wondering if it had been something he'd said or done. He'd meant every word he'd ever spoken to her, but maybe she didn't believe him when he said she made the sun rise and the earth spin, for him. When he'd told her that just by existing in his proximity, she set him free.

"Yo!" A familiar voice broke his reverie. "James, get in."

Drew pulled up and popped open the passenger-side door. Wordlessly, James stepped into the vehicle. After Estie had left, James had called Drew. His roommate had promised to pick James up, no questions asked, and get him back to the mountain in time for the afternoon shift. James might as well work; skiing would clear his head, as it always did.

"James. James!"

James startled slightly. "What?"

Drew stared at him. "Buckle up."

He reached for his seatbelt, strapping in as Drew drove out of the center of town and in the direction of the mountain.

"Are you… okay?"

"Drew…" James hoped the warning in his voice would be sufficient. It was not.

"No, I know I said I wouldn't ask, but, like… Are you okay?"

James stared at the dashboard. "Why wouldn't I be?" *Why hadn't Estie stayed?*

"Because you're the most safety-oriented person I've ever met, and somehow *I* had to tell you to put on your seatbelt just now?" Drew accelerated slightly. "Also, you took off work for the second time this week. And apparently you met up with some chick—"

"She's not *some chick*," James muttered.

Drew glanced over at him. "What?"

"Nothing. Keep your eyes on the road," James intoned.

His friend heaved a sigh. "Fine, but what are you going to tell the boss?"

James shrugged. "I told Eric I was sick. I'll just say I'm feeling better."

"He's not going to like—"

"It's spring break and the slopes are slick where they aren't icy. Eric needs every instructor he can get. He can't afford to chew me out for a miraculous recovery."

Drew nodded reluctantly. "Okay, but you better slap a smile on that surly face, because if not you'll scare all the students away."

James eyed his roommate. "What are you talking about?" He'd never been one to fake a smile, and his slight stoicism was a running joke among the other instructors.

"You've been grinning like a madman all week."

James snorted. "I have not."

"You've been smiling, at least."

Only because of Estie. Estie, who was on her way to the airport, or perhaps already in the air. And James was only just now realizing his mistake in letting her get away. Why, why hadn't he fought for her? Why hadn't he knelt on the cabin floor and begged her to stay?

"You'll probably be on babysitting duty, this afternoon." Drew referred to teaching kids as babysitting. Usually, James would have argued against the term, protested that his students were budding athletes who deserved to be taken seriously, but today… "There's a lot of young families this year."

James nodded absently. He'd rather work with kids, right now. Working with adults would remind him of Estie's absence; he already felt the lack of her keenly, like that first week of withdrawal. But he wouldn't be without her forever. She would call, soon. When she landed. She'd promised, hadn't she?

They pulled into the employee parking lot and made their way to the locker rooms. Eric was, as Drew had predicted, suspicious of James' remarkable recovery. But, as James had predicted, he was short staffed and in no position to get pissed.

James brought his phone with him, in his jacket, to teach the Level One kids. It didn't ring once, but then again she'd likely still be in the air. Montana to Boston was four hours and twenty minutes.

By the time he and Drew pulled into their usual parking spot at the little apartment complex, the phone still hadn't made a sound. James checked the side switch, to make sure the volume was on. And he unlocked it, and went through the call log. Nothing. Which made sense, because he hadn't felt or heard it ring. But it also didn't make sense, because she definitely should have landed by now. Maybe the luggage claim situation was dire? Or she was waiting until she'd gotten back from the airport, to her apartment. James could under-stand her wanting to wait until she had some privacy.

As the hours stretched on, however, he gradually ceased to under-stand. It was past ten, her time. She'd been home for hours, probably. Why hadn't she called him? Was something wrong? Or had she been planning to break her promise all along?

James went back over the week in his mind. He thought about their every interaction, from that first, fateful fall, to when she promised to call. He thought about the sound of her laughter, the dimple in her cheek, the scent of her shampoo, the satin of her inner thigh, and the star-like twinkle in her eye.

It was all so stunningly simple: he loved her. And he'd thought, he'd hoped—he now prayed—that she loved him, too. But she hadn't called, and he didn't have her number—not even her last name. There was nothing he could do. Had she planned this, too?

Night loomed, and James learned what it felt like for his heart to break.

CHAPTER 10
SKI BUM

On one side of Estie there was a pile of used tissues, on the other sat her older sister. Estie clutched her new phone, in its new and liquid-proof case, to her ear as she waited for someone, anyone to pick up.

"Blue Sky Resort, Winter Sports Office. How can I help you?"

Estie put on her sunniest, least waterlogged front. "Hi! This is Esther Williams, I've recently skied at your resort. I was wondering if you could help me—"

The man on the other end sighed. "Esther Williams, you said?"

Estie sat up a little straighter. "Yes?"

"Yeah, my colleague warned me about you. He said you called six times yesterday. I'm surprised your number isn't blocked from the system."

Estie deflated. "Oh."

His tone turned slightly more sympathetic, but nevertheless remained stern. "Listen, I don't know what your story is, and I don't particularly care. As my colleague no doubt told you, we don't give out our instructors' personal information to anyone, even former students. Especially former students." He paused. "You'd be surprised at how many crazies we get, calling up and demanding instructors' cell numbers. Safety first, you understand?"

"But—"

"*Don't* make me put you on the list," the man warned. "Now, you have a nice day."

"Please, sir, just—"

"Don't call again." The line went dead.

Estie let out a little sob, prompting Flo to rub soothing circles across her back.

"Come on, Estie. You're going to get put on a list, and then we'll never be able to go back there." Flo smoothed a strand of Estie's hair behind her ear. "Don't you want to go back next year, and see if your man's still working there?"

Estie shook her head. "I can't wait that long."

Flo sighed. "Then what are you going to do?"

"I'll think of something," she sniffed. "I'm a writer, ideas are what I do."

"That was fast," Flo remarked with uncharacteristic amazement. "I can't believe you wrote a book in three and a half months."

"Four," Estie corrected her sister. "Including the weeks I spent working on it with my editor while waiting for my illustrator to design a cover. And it's not like I did anything else during that time."

She'd stopped running, not that she'd ever really started. She'd stopped going out, not that she'd had many friends with whom to go out. Stopped online shopping when she was supposed to be drafting, stopped drinking on weeknights because she knew better, stopped answering emails except those related to her back catalogue. She'd even stopped scrolling through social media for hours at a time—because she wouldn't find him there, on a website or an app, much less at the bottom of a bottle of wine.

Wherever he was, he was utterly absent a presence online. After the people over at Blue Sky Resort had blocked her number, Estie had spent weeks scouring the internet for him, turning up not a single post or article or profile. She'd enlisted the help of family and friends, but even that mild humiliation proved pointless. Estie had been forced to accept that he was well and truly off the grid. Which... made sense, knowing him.

Because she did know him, for all that they'd spent less than a week together. She'd gotten to know him, and he'd gotten under her skin. Like the Sinatra song, absent its happy ending.

Estie wouldn't have a happy ending, herself. Probably not. But her characters would, characters she'd based—in a move that might have been slightly unethical, and definitely more than a little bit desperate—on herself and on him. Not exactly, though. She'd changed the color of his eyes, and his name. She'd changed the kind of covers he played. But his calm confidence, his stern stoicism, his unrepentant romanticism... those, she'd left the same.

This book was a testament to her enduring love for him. Testimony, too, before the court of the universe. Maybe the jury of the fates would hear her case and decide, as only they could, to put her once more on the same path as James.

James...

She never said his name, not anymore. It hurt too much. But the pain... she deserved it, didn't she? For leaving, on a jet plane. For abandoning him, without bothering to explain. Well, that last part hadn't been her fault. But she could have stowed her phone before—whatever. What a fool she'd been, and a coward, in the name of caution. Too much of a coward, too scared of commitment, to see her own Happily Ever After through. And she'd stolen his, too.

"Estie?" Flo's mildly concerned tone indicated that this was not the first time she'd said her sister's name. "Are you still with me?"

Estie sighed. "Yes, yes. Sorry. I'm ready." They were about to press the proverbial button, to launch her latest book. *Ski Bum*, she'd called it, a story about two strangers: a writer and her ski instructor, falling in love on the snowy slopes. The book was an apology, although James would likely never read it, as well as a Hail Mary—just in case he did.

"And you're sure about that... clue?" Her older sister was eyeing her warily.

Estie nodded, resolute. Because it worked in romance novels, didn't it? The grand gesture, the declaration of love, albeit a bit delayed? And even if it didn't work, it couldn't hurt. It was only a line at the end of the acknowledgments—a dedication would have felt stalkerish, she'd figured as she had flipped through the front matter for the thousandth time.

"I just wonder..." Flo nibbled her lower lip. "I'm not sure I should encourage it, this mad hope. You don't need more disappointment."

Estie straightened in her seat, tearing her eyes from the computer's screen. "Hope isn't mad, Flo. Or maybe it is, but who cares? I fucked up, royally. I fell in love and instead of following that love, instead of facing him and fessing up, I... I ran away." She locked eyes with her sister. "I made a mistake that I know I probably can't rectify. But I can still try."

"Why? Estie, it's not logical—"

"*Love* isn't logical. You know that. And I love James. I loved him after six days of knowing him. And I still love him, after all these months apart. And if there's even the slightest chance that he reads what I wrote... Listen, I know you don't read a lot of romance, so you wouldn't necessarily know. But romance novels are about hope. And trust, and faith, and perseverance. They're about putting yourself out there, trying your best, and trusting that the universe bends towards love, however long the arc." She paused. "I want to replicate that resilience, honor that hope."

Flo smiled, reluctantly. "I *hope* you've written that little speech down, sis."

"Why?"

Flo's smile widened into a grin. "For when this book becomes a bestseller, and you're asked to speak on panels at bookshops and conferences."

Estie laughed in dubious disbelief, but still squeezed her sister's hand. "Thanks for having faith in me, Flo."

"Of course." Flo guided Estie's hand toward the trackpad of her laptop. "Now, let's publish this bitc—book. Let's publish this book."

As he stared out at the Atlantic Ocean, James regretted having told his coworker and friend, Valerie, about the romance novelist he'd fallen in l—with whom he'd had a flirtation, months earlier. A flirtation that was haunting him, even now, months and months after its abrupt end. After he gave her his number and she never called or even texted him. Not even to tell him that their affair had come to an end.

He especially regretted it ever since Valerie had asked him Estie's name and pen name and sub-genre. Apparently, his coworker was an avid reader in the romance genre. Well, Estie hadn't told him anything more than her first name, perhaps out of a desire for privacy, perhaps because she wanted to keep some small piece of her hidden, hers, when everything else had been fair game between them—because they'd shared everything. Even a soul, James thought, sometimes, when he was feeling especially sorry for himself. A soul, like Aristophanes had said. Two people, divided by the gods, destined to search for one another: each for the missing half of them that was the other.

Well, they'd found each other. And been divided again. But not by the gods. By her.

He'd failed, in his optimism, to see that rejection coming. And yet, he couldn't bring himself to hate her. Because he loved her, still. Now and forever.

James had thought Valerie had given up the hunt for Estie, however, as she'd gone quiet for a few days. In peace, at last, they went to work each day, teaching the kids whose families lived and summered on the little island to sail. If one could wrangle ten seven-year-olds in sailboats "in peace." It was more like war.

There were collisions, of course: boats hitting other boats or (hollow) booms hitting (equally hollow) heads. There were unexpected jibes and lost lines and the occasional capsize—even one alarming death-roll. There were tears and tantrums, pranks and pushing each other in. Well, not the instructors. They were supposed to be above all that.

War, it was. But James would willingly call it peace, because there weren't any invasive questions about his life, his sex life, or even—he might as well call it what it had been—his love life. From Valerie, that was.

The students, who were naturally curious and just a bit devious, pestered him with many an inappropriate or invasive inquiry. They'd picked up on his heartbreak, somehow, probably using some form of emotional radar or interpersonal sonar. James was starting to think they'd all been born with antennae, so astute were their questions, so accurate their conclusions. Children. They hadn't used to terrify him.

But James could handle children. It was, after all, his job. Winter and summer. On the slopes or in the water. What he couldn't handle was Valerie, sticking her nose where it didn't belong. One of these days, if she kept needling him, he was going to lose it, again, and it would be worse this time because this time, unlike the previous hundred times, he would lose it in another person's company, in broad daylight—usually, he kept it together until he was alone in the room he rented, above the empty gift shop, in the middle of the night.

Which was why, when Valerie looked up from her tablet and cleared her throat with a delicacy that could only be portentous of questions to come, James sat up in alarm.

It was their afternoon off and they were dangling their feet in the frigid and slightly oil-slick water off the end of the public dock. Valerie had been reading a book she'd downloaded instead of scrolling social media, because the yacht club's wifi didn't reach the end of the dock. James had been lost in thought—memory, rather, of coffee-brown eyes and an unraveling red plait and a vintage ski suit whose cuffs were a little frayed. But when Valerie surfaced, and made that hesitant sound, James snapped out of his reverie and back into reality.

"What is it?"

"Yeesh, that tone! So severe. I hope you don't use it on the students."

James leveled Valerie with a look. Or at least attempted to do so. She was now immune to his icy glares, after two months of them and six whole summers of his so-called stoicism before that. "Are you about to pry? I won't answer any more questions."

"Actually," Valerie announced with smug smile and an unnecessary display of pride, "I wasn't going to pry."

"What do you want, then?" She'd interrupted a perfectly pleasant, if masochistic, walk down memory lane. He'd been remembering that first day.

"I want you to listen to a passage from a book I've spent the past couple of days reading. It was an instant bestseller, apparently. Published less than a month ago, and it was something of a surprise when it was announced, but now it's on all the lists."

James' own, wholly figurative, antenna pinged a warning. "Why?"

Valerie leaned in. James didn't like the excited gleam in her eye. A little breathlessly, with an air of confession, she whispered, "I've found her."

James had thought he'd been sitting up straight, before. Now, though, his spine truly snapped to rigid attention. His mother would have been proud of his posture. "What?"

"Well," Valerie glanced at her tablet. "How do I put this?" She frowned, and then it must have come to her, because she grinned. "I think, actually, it would be better to say… I've found *you*."

"I don't appreciate the wordplay, Valerie." James tried to sound bored, but his heart was beating faster than it had in months—faster than it had since he'd first seen *her*. Since he'd last made love to her, rather.

Love…

It had been love, and he'd known it—they'd both known it, felt it, lived it—and yet that hadn't been enough for her. She'd still left him.

James' fist curled in rage and hurt and frustration.

"This book I'm reading, James, it's… the plot is exactly the same as the story you told me, about the woman you met in Montana. About the woman you fell in love with, who left. Only, in this, she doesn't leave. She considers it, sure, but then he confesses his love for her. He fights for her. And she stays."

James glared at the water that was gently lapping his ankles, but he was grateful for its frigid grip. If it weren't for the grounding effect of the cold Maine water… he'd currently be losing it. "So it's my fault, is what you're saying. If I had fought for her, she would have stayed." Except she wouldn't have. Even if he'd fought for her, she'd already made up her mind to get on that plane.

That's what he knew, that's what he thought, that's why he hadn't fought. That, and the fact that he'd assumed she'd call. He'd given her his number, after all.

James wondered, not for the first time, when that decision—the one to leave him, without a word's explanation—had been made. After he'd eaten her out on the side of a mountain? Had she regretted their recklessness? Before they'd made love—not fucked, that crass word couldn't possibly encompass what they'd experienced, in and around and alongside each other—or after? He'd fallen asleep first... Had she watched him sleep, and then made up her mind?

Or was he being too generous? Had she known all along, that she would love him and leave him? Because he knew—what he felt, he hadn't felt it alone. *She'd loved him, too.* But if she'd loved him, why had she left him? And not just why, *how* could she have done it? Walked out of that cabin, gotten on that plane, broke his heart in fucking twain? He'd loved her, and she'd loved him, but the latter love, her love—maybe it hadn't been the same. Maybe it hadn't been enough...

"No, James, that's not what—" Valerie huffed a sigh. "Just listen to this one passage, okay? Please?"

"Why?" James barely managed the word; his voice was near to shaking and his vision was already blurred.

"Because I think she regrets it."

His head whipped around and he stared, stunned, at his coworker. "Loving me? She regrets loving me?" It hurt, physically, the possibility. It hurt worse than heartbreak had. And the hurt was followed by horror. Had *he* somehow hurt *her*? Had he done something to make her regret their time together? Was this, in addition to everything, *his fault*?

Valerie rolled her eyes, possibly reading his mind. "No, you tit. She regrets leaving you. I think—I think she still loves you, and this book... it's her way of telling you."

James forced himself to turn away from Valerie, from her unspoken promises and her dangerous words. Words which he oh-so-desperately wanted to hear from another woman's lips—pink, they were, plush and perfect for kissing...

He kicked the half-submerged float with his heel, wincing when the little mussels growing there, amidst the seaweed, cracked under the force of his foot. Their broken shells scraped and stabbed his calloused skin.

"Just, listen to this. For me, for you, for Elizabeth Brooks."

James squinted at Valerie in confusion, and because of the bright golden rays of the now setting sun. It was beautiful, sure, but it had nothing on the dawn. At least, not when that dawn was breaking across Estie's naked body, painting her pink as her cheeks when he complimented her, pink as her lips when he kissed her, pink as her labia when he licked her…

Valerie's voice intruded on the fantasy. "I'd call her by her real name," she continued, pointedly, "but you never told me her real name."

"Estie," he whispered, letting the light wind carry the word away from him. And yet, she never left him. How could she? When she lived in the hollow of his heart?

"Estie," Valerie repeated. "Right, well, listen to what Estie has to say about you, James."

James nodded slowly, finding himself strangely free of willful resistance at the moment. Perhaps it was the fact that he'd finally shared Estie's name with someone other than the silent trees and the summer's breeze.

Valerie cleared her throat again, this time with a kind of calm confidence. And then she began to read.

"*I love Montana. I love the mountains, most of all, but the valleys, too. And the rivers, the bubbling brooks. I love the flowers peeping through the spring snow. The* centaurea montana, *that's my favorite variety. And I love the ice, just not when it covers the roads.*"

Valerie paused, looking up at James, concern written all over her face.

"Keep going," he said, his voice hoarse with need. He needed Estie; after all this time, he still needed her—he would always need her. But, right now, all that was on offer was her words. Because they were her words, without a doubt. He'd know that voice anywhere.

"*Natalie Maines had it right. I needed these wide open spaces. I needed the freedom to leave my old life behind and find myself in open skies, and in his open arms. Because more than mountains or the state of Montana, I love* him. *His eyes, his lips, the way his stern expression sometimes slips. I love his mind and the way he moves, his lean muscles and the buckles on his big ski boots. His smile, like the sun coming out from behind a pensive cloud. His*" laughter, like the low rumble of far-off thunder that signals the end of a desperate drought."

Wet, hot tears had started to stream down James' cheeks. One made its way to his lips, which he licked, finding them salty yet sweet. With a slight tang that he suspected was runoff sunscreen. He looked at Valerie, who had paused, again, her own eyes wide and a little watery. He nodded, and she started to read the rest of the passage.

"I love him and, now that I've found him, I'll never leave him. We'll travel the world together, or at least the country. It's the seasonal life, for me. For us. Because it's us, now. And forever."

James suddenly swung his legs up onto the dock, not thinking, just moving. Going to Estie, to the nearest approximation of her. He tore the tablet from Valerie's unresisting hands, ignoring her slack jaw, her look of shock and slight alarm.

James' eyes focused on the tablet's screen. He scanned the page, drinking in Estie's words like they were milk and honey. Because this love was the land that was promised, and these words—to him, they were sacred, a covenant of a kind. He didn't care how many others had read them, her unspoken declaration. She'd written them for his eyes only. She might as well be standing there, whispering them in his ear. He could hear her. He could feel her.

I think, maybe, we were meant to be. Two halves, one whole. His is my soul. And to think, that I almost didn't go on that trip to Blue Sky. To think that I almost never met the love of my life.

The chapter ended, the page went blank. But James' mind started whirring. The gears, the cogs, the machinery of his heart—it all started turning. And it stopped feeling like machinery, frankly. Because, after five months' atrophy, five months' agony...

James had Estie. And he'd never be without her again.

He flipped back to the beginning of the e-book. There was no dedication; the front matter failed him. He scrolled to the end, to the acknowledgements and started to scan them. Surely, surely, she had made some mention of... There! At the very end.

Finally, I'd like to thank James, who taught me how to ski—and how to love. I've lost you, James. Find me?

James looked up at Valerie, his eyes wide and no doubt wild as he was now feeling. "You have to help me, Valerie."

Valerie nodded slowly, alarm fading into awe and understanding. When she spoke, her voice was steady, calm. Resolute. There was the steadfast sailor he knew. "What do you need me to do?"

CHAPTER 11
ELIZABETH BROOKS

ALONE IN THE backroom of the bookstore, Estie checked her phone, still safe in its new waterproof case. Well, she'd bought the case six months ago, so maybe it wasn't new. But she didn't want to acknowledge the passage of time, the fact that every day carried her further away from *his* embrace.

"Elizabeth?" An unfamiliar voice called her pen name. Estie didn't register it at first, despite the fact that she was on high alert. Today was a big day; she was being publicly interviewed—in person, although there would be a livestream. "Elizabeth Brooks?"

Estie turned, looking up from her phone. A woman wearing slacks and a warm smile was standing in the doorway. Estie pushed off the wall of paperback preorders against which she'd been leaning. Soon enough, thanks to the print run she had ordered in the wake of her latest novel's success, the backroom of the Beacon Hill bookstore would be stocked with stacks of *Ski Bum*. "Genevieve Clark?"

"That's me! And, I assume, since no one but staff and speakers are permitted in the backroom, that you're you?"

Estie held out her hand, flashing the woman a friendly smile. "Call me Elizabeth. And it's a pleasure to meet you. I liked your article, by the way, in the Globe." She struggled to recall the title. "On the art of the clinch."

Genevieve's face lit up. "Oh! You've read my work!" She smiled conspiratorially, lowering her voice slightly. "My interest in vintage covers isn't purely academic, as that article may have lead you to believe."

Estie laughed. "Whose is?"

"All those buxom, breathless babes... Talk about an awakening for pre-teen me, when I first discovered my mother's hidden Woodiwiss collection!" Genevieve grinned. "I love romance as much as the next reader, which is why I'm so excited to be interviewing you today!" Her expression grew serious. "Honestly, though, *Ski Bum* is spectacular. As the sales reflect! Congratulations on hitting all the lists! And on the upcoming print run! Very exciting news."

Estie tried and failed to suppress a giddy grin. It was all so surreal: the critical success of her book, its widespread reception by avid and casual readers of romance—and the earnings were nice, too. It was altogether almost enough to fill the James-sized hole in her heart. Almost. For an hour or so—for the length of this interview, at least. "I still can't believe it," she confessed, forcing her mind back to *Ski Bum*'s success.

"Well, having read it three times, and not just because I wanted to be prepared for this interview, I can." Genevieve checked her watch. "We should get out there, get started. The bulk of the seats were already filled, when I arrived. You should have charged for admission!"

"It wouldn't have been fair, since we're live-streaming."

"True." Genevieve gestured toward the door.

"After you!" Estie did a brief breathing exercise, then followed Genevieve out of the back and into the bookstore's main room. Shelves had been moved to make space for chairs as well as a standing section at the back. All but two seats were taken, the two seats that were reserved for Estie and Genevieve, and the standing section at the back was, to Estie's surprise and daunted delight, positively packed. Most everyone was holding a signed bookplate or one of the bookmarks she'd had printed with a slimmer version of the cover design.

"Friends, neighbors, romance readers..." Genevieve began, "Please join me in welcoming the author of the summer's biggest hit—as well as a sizable backlist—the one, the only: Elizabeth Brooks."

Estie blushed profusely, probably turning red as a beet—or a particularly ruddy carrot, what with her hair—as the room erupted into applause. She accepted the microphone which Genevieve then handed her, as the other woman signaled with raised eyebrows and a nod in the direction of the audience that it was time for her to say hello.

Once the applause had faded into a few straggling claps, Estie cleared her throat and spoke. "Hi!" Her voice came out unnaturally high. She cleared her throat again and focused on her sister, who was standing off to one side. "Er, hello."

Flo smiled encouragingly. Freddy, standing beside their older sister with his boyfriend, grinned wickedly and mouthed something rude. Estie refrained from rolling her eyes, but felt some of the confidence she'd had earlier, when practicing in front of her mirror, return. She addressed the audience again.

"It's an honor to be here, at my favorite bookstore, with all of you. I can't tell you how much this means to me. *Ski Bum* is perhaps the book that's closest to my heart, and sharing it with the world was hard. But the fact that you all read it, connected with its characters, and—I hope —found meaning, to say nothing of a message, within its pages…" She took a deep breath. "Thank you, all of you."

"And thank you, Elizabeth, for giving us the gift that is your writing." Genevieve beamed at the audience, who were clapping again. "Now, I have a couple of questions for you, Elizabeth, and then, if we have time, we'll open it up to the audience before you begin to sign."

Estie pretty much blacked out for the entirety of the interview. Her anxiety was through the roof, and it was all she could do to answer Genevieve's questions in full sentences. But by the time the audience Q&A rolled around, she was feeling calmer. In part thanks to the faces Freddy kept pulling, which made her want to laugh and roll her eyes and, occasionally, toss a book at his head. Little brothers were annoying, but they had their uses. Estie was amazed to find that Freddy worked almost as well as clonazepam, albeit via a totally different neural pathway, to lower her heart rate and help her focus on her words.

The majority of the questions from the audience were softballs: what kind of writer was she (pantser), did she type or handwrite (Estie held up her fingers to demonstrate the conspicuous absence of ink splatter), would she ever write in a different genre (never say never, but... no, never), et cetera. There was one tricky one (did she ever base her writing on her own experiences, which Estie struggled to answer honestly, the words lodging in her throat and tears, to her shame and surprise, coming fast to her eyes; ultimately she had to be rescued by Genevieve, who said something witty about ethics and the muse) and then, Estie thought, they were done.

Except that, as the audience's laughter faded into faint whispers, a tall man with long, dark hair and a thick mustache, standing in the far back where Estie had only ever glanced, raised his hand.

Estie's heart did a little skip and skittered, gaining speed again. She took a grounding breath and reflected that she really did need to get glasses because her eyes were playing tricks on her, no doubt due to the combination of dehydration and the lithium in her system. The man, he looked an awful lot like... But no, that was impossible. That couldn't be—

Genevieve stepped in, since Estie was clearly out of commission. "In the back, do you have a question? We only have time for a quick-ie." She smiled apologetically.

The man nodded, and accepted the mic that was being passed through the small crowd. He held it up to his lips and when he spoke, the tenor of his voice was achingly familiar. "Just the one." Then he looked directly at Estie, his eyes bright and the color of moss in the moonlight. Estie couldn't breathe, because she knew that hue. "Did you mean what you wrote, when you asked me to find you?"

Estie wasn't entirely sure what happened next. She stood and she might have dropped the mic in the process, but not before it picked up her gasping his name, loud enough for the audience to wince. But Estie didn't care. The only thing that mattered was that he had found her. Her ski instructor in shining armor.

James. He was here.

The microphone Estie had been holding didn't like being dropped, but James didn't give a damn. He handed his own mic to a nearby fan. And then Estie was moving, and the small crowd was parting like the Red Sea. Ready to carry James and Estie into each other's arms, into joy and peace and safety.

Just as Estie reached him, however, just as she looked ready to launch herself into his waiting arms, her eyes widened and her own arms flailed. James leapt forward without a moment's hesitation, his instincts spurring him on. He caught her before she could hit the carpet, clutching her to him like she was the most important person, the only person, in the world for him. Because she was, and she always would be.

Safe in his arms, secure in his embrace, Estie—started laughing?

James frowned, still supporting her weight. "Why are you laughing?"

She just shook her head, still laughing although now tears were starting to stream down her cheeks.

James' frown deepened with his concern. "Why are you crying?" He asked, in a softer voice.

"I'm crying because I'm laughing, you dingbat! And I'm laughing because this is the way we met!" She started to hiccup, removing one hand from his shoulder to wipe her eyes. "Oh, just—help me up?"

James shook his head. "I have a better idea." And then he leaned down, gathering her close, and kissed her like he should have, like he'd wanted to, that first day on the mountain. He kissed her with every ounce of pent up emotion he'd been holding in his heart, for so many months. With his hope and his fear and his hurt and his joy and his lust and his love—above all, love. Because he'd never told her, but she had to know.

James pulled back, but not before Estie darted forward and pressed another, quicker, kiss to his lips. Smiling, grinning, beaming, he stared deep into her eyes and whispered, "I love you, Estie."

Apparently, his whisper was loud enough for the crowd to hear, or perhaps his mic was nearby and picked it up, because the room erupted in cheers.

James hauled Estie to her feet.

She smiled at him, her eyes watery and a little red with tears shed and still unshed. "I love you, too. And I should have told you, as soon as I knew. But I was on a plane, and then there was breastmilk all over my phone, and—"

James' forehead furrowed. "What?"

Estie huffed a laugh. Then hiccuped. "I'm sorry, James. I'm so, so sorry."

"I—You don't have to apologize, Estie. Just… maybe explain?"

She nodded fervently, her brown eyes wide. "Can we go somewhere, and talk?" She glanced around, and James followed suit, suddenly noticing all the phones and cameras in the room. Then, giggling, she glanced back at him. "I think they live-streamed that kiss."

James assessed the situation as best he could, his head still muddled with a mess of emotions. He knew that Estie was a private person, despite her typically brazen attitude. He also knew that social media was a minefield. "Do you mind?"

Estie shook her head, smiling. "No, not unless you do. Do you?"

James didn't give a damn. Still, as much as he wanted to continue to make out with Estie, he very much needed to talk to her. And he'd prefer that their conversation not be tweeted all over TikTok, or whatever. "Let's get out of here."

Estie took his hand. "I know a place we can go, so long as you promise not to judge me for not having put away my laundry."

James chuckled, feeling a weight lift. He was free, like he always was with Estie. "Lead the way."

They didn't talk, not on the walk to Estie's apartment, and not after they arrived—unless one counted the various murmured questions and cries and verbal caresses that came, part and parcel, with sex. It was as though they needed the silence, to ease back into each other's presence after such a long absence. And as they lay, entwined, on her queen sized bed in her studio apartment in September's lingering heat, they were quiet, too. Until Estie realized she had something rather important to say, before the mood faded and they lost track of love during the inevitable post-coital negotiation of logistics.

"I love you, James."

He smiled into the side of her breast, where he had burrowed. "I love you, too, Estie. More than anything, or anyone, in this world."

She took a deep breath: engaging her diaphragm on the inhale, counting the exhale. "I feel like, all my life, I've been collecting little crumbs of connection—sustaining myself on mere morsels alone." Her voice shook slightly as she spoke, and James raised himself on one elbow, watching her. "It's not enough, anymore," she continued, staring at a small crack in the ceiling. "I want more." She took another deep breath, this time not bothering to count but instead drinking in the rich scent of his skin, of his sweat. And pine needles, which she'd forgotten about. Probably some hyper-organic soap made in Maine or Montana alone. At last, she met his eyes. "I want *you*."

"You can have me," he said immediately, resolutely. "I don't care what it takes. I'll quit my job, I'll go back to school, get that software engineering degree." He sat up, shaking the hair out of his eager eyes. "I'll move to Boston and ski on the weekends, like a regular person. I'll give up the travel, the seasonal work. I'll find something steady, to sustain me. To sustain *us*. Because it's us, now. And forever."

Estie shook her head as she, too, pushed up from her place among the pillows. "As happy as I am to hear you quote my book-shaped apology back to me... That doesn't make sense, James. I don't want you to give that much up for me."

He stiffened, probably anticipating rejection. It wouldn't be the first time he felt it from her, she thought, wincing. "Then what are we supposed to do? When will I ever see you? On holidays? For spring break? I can't—" His voice broke, and Estie's hand automatically came up to cradle his face, but he brushed her away. "I can't live like that. Without you. That's the one thing, the only thing, I won't do. Not now that I've already had to..."

"Hey, hey. No black and white thinking, as my therapist would say."

"I know, I know. That's what my sponsor used to tell me." He frowned. "Apparently I have a tendency."

"Well, your sponsor and my therapist would probably agree on a lot of things. And you do—have a tendency, that is. But so do I." She cupped his chin and coaxed him into meeting her eyes. "Listen. I can't live without you, either. That's not what I'm proposing."

His frown deepened, that stern expression returning, replacing some of the fear she'd seen in his eyes with skepticism. "Then what exactly are you proposing?"

"That we walk the middle path. Together."

His eyes narrowed slightly with suspicion, but he bade her, "Go on."

Estie took a moment to ground herself. Then, she told him her plan. The one she'd been formulating ever since she let herself hope that he would find her again. "I'll move to Montana." He shook his head, but she kept going. "We'll get an apartment together—we can afford it, the two of us, together. And my parents would be willing to help. If you're open to that." She bit her lip, belatedly realizing that not everyone accepted financial assistance as readily as she did.

"That's fine. I wouldn't mind the help, if that's what you're worried about, but... Your whole life is here, Estie. I can't—I can't steal you away from your family, your friends, your future..."

"I'm not done, James." She smiled at him, softening the reprimand. "I've been doing a little research," she confessed. "The ski season starts in October and ends in April. During that time, we'd live in Montana, or wherever work takes you. It doesn't matter to me, because I work remotely. I don't even need wifi!"

He raised one dark brow.

"Well, I will, for research. And procrastinating on social media, keeping up with what few friends I have. But that's beside the point. I can write from wherever. In fact, my writing will probably be better, because I'll have seen more of the world than my small corner!" She took a steadying breath. "I've always wanted to travel more, James. To see the world, or even just the country."

James' frown had softened, but only slightly. "What about your friends, your family? Won't you miss them?"

"First of all, as I said, I don't really have that many friends. God's honest truth. Second, that's what phones are for, James. I can text, or call, or video call, whenever. And if I need to see my family, face to face… You know my siblings love to ski. And my parents? Now that they're retired, they're *really* into the idea of taking regular trips cross-country."

James' brow furrowed. "You've spoken to them about this?"

Estie shrugged, smiling shyly. "I may have introduced the idea to them hypothetically."

"But you didn't—you couldn't have known I'd find you."

"Which is why everyone cautioned me against hope. But… I had faith in you. And nothing to lose."

James shook his head, his features contorted by hurt and confusion. "If I hadn't found you, if you'd gotten your hopes up for nothing… Wouldn't that have broken your heart, Estie? How could you do that to yourself?"

Estie tried to wipe surreptitiously at a tear that had gathered in her eye. James intercepted her hand, replacing her fingers with the calloused pad of his thumb. Estie struggled to hold it together, but ultimately settled for being held as James' hand lingered, caressing her increasingly damp cheek. "My heart was already broken, James. It's like I said… Already having lost you, I had nothing left to lose."

James cradled her face a moment longer, then wordlessly pulled her into his arms. They sat like that for a few minutes, as Estie allowed her emotions to settle once more. "I'm never leaving you again," James said, finally. "I'll do it, this plan of yours. Whatever it is, whatever it takes. No more heartbreak."

Estie shook her head, smiling into James' bicep. "You haven't even heard the rest of the plan, James."

"I don't need to," he said, his voice muffled by her hair, which was in a shocking state of disrepair. But Estie didn't care. James heaved a sigh and pulled back, holding her in his capable hands. "But I'll let you explain it to me, because—and I want you to remember this—I will always listen to you."

"You better," she teased. "I'm a genius and this plan is going to knock your socks off!"

He shifted to gesture to his bare feet. Wiggling his toes, he returned with solemnity that wasn't entirely sincere, "It already has."

Estie pushed at him playfully, and they fell back to the bed, a tangle of naked limbs and laughter. A few minutes later, however, she pushed him onto his back, all business. Straddling him, she announced, "Now, I'm going to tell you my plan for the off-season, which involves your finding a sailing gig near Boston, so I can spend the summer here. And then," she added, rolling her hips just right, "I'm going to ride you so hard you forget my plan, and have to ask me to tell you again."

His cock twitched against her swollen clit and Estie bit back a moan. "Better idea," James growled. "We'll multitask." And then, lifting her by the waist, he dragged himself along her folds until he was notched, ready at her entrance. Slowly, steadily, he eased his way in. Estie's gasp grew into a groan of pleasure. "Remember how you fell, that first day?" He drew her down and near.

Estie sank onto him, letting him deeper, deeper, deeper… "I didn't —oh!—fall." He'd bottomed out, and it was bliss.

James rolled his eyes, or maybe they rolled back in pleasure. Estie wasn't sure anymore. She wasn't sure of anything, except that she loved him and he loved her. "You fell," he panted, pinching her left nipple. "But I fell harder."

Without waiting for her response, James started to thrust and it was just—exactly right, and also too much. Estie threw her head back in ecstasy and surrendered to love's infinity.

CHAPTER 12
BRUNCH

"JAMES." Estie didn't bother to open her eyes; from behind closed lids, she could already tell it was bright. She could also tell that someone was in the kitchen, trying and failing to be quiet. A pan knocked against another pan. "James, what are you doing?"

"Making breakfast. Go back to sleep, Estie."

Estie hauled herself up on one elbow, still not opening her eyes. There was hair in her mouth, and she definitely looked a fright. "I usually just have a yogurt," she yawned as the stove clicked to life.

An eggshell cracked. "I need something with a bit more protein. Go back to sleep, baby."

Estie smiled, at last opening her eyes and immediately squinting in the bright morning light. "I had forgotten—I like it when you call me 'baby.'"

James was standing, stark naked but for a frilly apron her sister had sewn her years ago, in a pool of sunlight in front of the stove. With bedhead to rival the frontrunner of a boyband, he looked like a disheveled angel. But not a biblically accurate one, thank heaven. "Noted. Baby."

Estie grinned, throwing her bare legs over the side of the bed and stretching her arms way up in the air. "Nobody's putting me in the corner!" Then she resumed ogling James' ass, which she hadn't initially given its proper attention. Skiing was a sport, and his backside confirmed it.

James glanced curiously at her over his shoulder.

"Relax, darling, I'm just admiring your glutes." She waggled her eyebrows at him.

He shook his head, his brow furrowing. "It's not that. What do you mean, put you in the corner? I'm not familiar with that expression."

Estie's jaw dropped. "You've never seen *Dirty Dancing*?" James shook his head again, then returned his attention to the frying pan, whose contents were starting to sizzle. "Not *Dirty Dancing*, not *The Princess Bride*... Have you even *lived*?"

He laughed, dryly, at that. "Not until I met you."

Estie's heart flip-flopped. "It's a movie," she explained. "A coming of age story. It has *everything*." She slid out of bed and started to search for her robe, which was never on its hook. "Sex, love, dancing, montages, weirdly shaped watermelons, Patrick Swayze and Jennifer Grey, an abortion, the Catskills, and that song—"

"Time of My Life?"

"No, Hungry Eyes." She stopped rummaging through the pile of clothes that had been on her bed and were now, as a result of her kicking them unceremoniously off it mid-sex, on the floor. She turned and narrowed her eyes at him. "I thought you said you hadn't seen it."

He shrugged, poking his eggs with a spatula. "I haven't. But I think I've seen a clip." He glanced at her over his shoulder. "Does he lift her up?"

"Yes!" Estie clapped her hands together. "You'll love it. I know because I love it. Everyone loves it. Except, probably, Republicans."

James chuckled. "Where are the plates?"

"In the cabinet next to the fridge." She tossed the pile of clothes back on the bed. "The better question is, where is my robe?"

A plate clattered as he pulled it from the stack. "Is it pink?"

Estie spun around. "How did you know?"

James shrugged. "I think I saw it hanging on a hook. Over there." He gestured with the plate towards the closet, which was open. Sure enough, hanging from a hook she'd proudly if unevenly screwed into the wooden door herself, was her robe. Estie shook her head in amazement and wrapped it around her naked body, which was gloriously sore.

Standing with his back to the stove, James frowned.

"What? What's wrong?" Estie knotted the sash at her natural waist.

"Nothing. I just didn't get much of a chance to admire *your* glutes, since I was busy cooking breakfast." He sounded slightly forlorn.

Estie couldn't help it. She laughed. "What glutes? Besides, we have the rest of our lives."

Sudden awe lit James' eyes, which were a clear, verdant green in the morning light. He stared at her for a long moment, his lips parted. Then he smiled. "You're right. Are you sure you don't want any of this?"

She shook her head. "I have to take my morning meds on an empty stomach. I'll eat in a bit." Then she crossed over to the kitchen, slid an arm around his neck, and pulled him down for a slow, toe-curling kiss. Which was marred, slightly, by the fact that she had morning breath. "I'll be right back," she said, grimacing.

But before she could dart off to the bathroom, James caught her by the wrist and reeled her back in for another knee-buckling kiss. She could taste the peppermint of her toothpaste on his lips. "Brush your teeth and take your meds, but come right back. No dawdling." He smacked her ass.

Estie gasped, delighted by this unexpected bossiness. Well, not entirely unexpected. The man taught for a living. She leaned in and nudged his chin with her nose. "Why?" She teased, "Because you'll miss me?"

He smiled, wickedly, and Estie felt a tingle between her legs despite the slight lingering soreness. James gestured to the plate of eggs he'd been holding throughout both kisses. "No, because I'm hungry. But my mother raised me right, and it would be rude to eat without you." His smile softened as he added, "*Baby*."

Estie snorted. Then she scurried off to the bathroom to perform the aforementioned ablutions.

"Oh, and Estie?"

She tossed her thyroid and anxiety medications back in one fell swallow, along with her Vitamin D. "Yes, James?"

"Are your parents in town?"

Estie squeezed toothpaste onto the faded bristles of her toothbrush. It was time to replace the piece of plastic. "Yes, they live here. Why?"

"I'd like to meet them."

Around the toothbrush, Estie managed, "Again? You've already met them."

"As your ski instructor, sure. But I want to get to know them. As your boyfriend."

Estie spat into the sink.

"I hope that's not your way of signaling disgust or disagreement," James joked. She could tell now, most of the time, when the deadpan was humorous and when he was serious.

Estie rinsed out the basin and the brush, replacing the latter in its little holder. "No, I think it's a lovely idea. I'm sure Flo's already told them the news of our reunion." She'd set her phone to silent as soon as she and James had arrived at her apartment. "In fact, it's probably all over Twitter." Estie exited the bathroom to find James perched on the couch—she didn't have the space for chairs or a kitchen table.

"Ah, yes, social media. Should I make some accounts?"

Estie thought about it. Then she lowered herself onto the couch beside him, inhaling his slightly sweaty, sexed up scent. "Mmm. No, you shouldn't. I like that you're my mystery man."

He set the eggs on the floor then practically pulled her into his lap. They kissed, lazily at first, then with a kind of starving vigor. James tasted like her toothpaste and himself, and Estie found that the combination was her new favorite flavor. She let her legs fall to either side, grinding against his growing erection. The only thing preventing his cock from pressing against her cunt was that fucking apron.

"Take it off," she moaned against his lips.

"What? Oh." He fumbled behind him for the apron's strings. But before he could free himself, and his long, thick, throbbing, and—frankly—beautiful dick, of the frilly little thing, his stomach gave an enormous growl.

"Oh, for fuck's sake," she sighed, slipping off his lap and back onto the couch. "Eat your breakfast."

James chuckled, a slightly sexually frustrated sound. "Will do."

"Meanwhile, I'll text my parents." Estie got up off the couch and started looking around the apartment for her phone. Usually, she let it charge overnight. But last night… Well, she'd been busy.

Looking up from the plate of eggs he was scarfing down like a man starved, James offered, "Have you checked under the bed?"

"Why would it be under the bed?"

He shrugged. "I think I heard it fall off the bed, in the middle of, you know," he gestured vaguely.

"Fucking each other's brains out?"

"If you like. So, yeah, maybe one of us kicked it under. In the process of fucking the other's brains out."

Estie frowned thoughtfully. "Well, it's as good a lead as any." She strode over to the bed and got down on her hands and knees to peer under the mattress. "Huh. Would you look at that." Her phone was a little dusty, but the screen wasn't even cracked. "You're a genius at finding things, did you know that?"

Blushing faintly, he smiled that rare, special smile of his. "Well, I found you, didn't I?"

"Estie, baby, it's time to go."

His girlfriend—god, that sounded nice—his girlfriend untied and retied her wrap dress. "Do I look alright?"

"No, you look beautiful. You are beautiful. And you are also the slowest dresser I have ever known. We're going to be late." James checked his watch, and indeed it was past noon. "Brunch is going to be lunch, if we don't leave soon."

Estie twirled in front of the mirror, then applied some lip balm. "Relax, James. Brunch can be as late as four in the afternoon. And besides, my family is used to my being late."

He shook his head and handed her her phone. "Not anymore. Not on my watch. I want to make a good second impression."

She rolled her eyes and tucked her phone into her purse. "Considering that your first impression was you singing Randy Travis up on a stage, I think you're okay." Picking up her keys, she paused. "And how many slow dressers have you known?"

James chuckled, feeling light and free. "Why? Are you going to slutshame me?"

"Oh, hush up. We're going to be late."

"That's my line!" But, dutifully, James followed his girlfriend out of her apartment and down the stairs.

They arrived at the restaurant before the majority of Estie's family, to James' initial surprise. But then he reconsidered, remembering that punctuality or a lack thereof tended to run in families. Nature or nurture, he wasn't sure.

The hostess lead them to the back of the restaurant, where glass doors opened onto a sunlit patio. Florence and her fiancé were already seated at a table there.

"Estie!"

"Flo!"

Estie's older sister smirked. "I see you've brought your boyfriend. At least, I hope he's your boyfriend, because the whole of the internet thinks he is. And if he's not, he's crashing family brunch."

Estie laughed. "Way to steal my thunder, sis. Yes, James is my boyfriend." She linked arms with him, looking up. "Aren't you, my love?"

James kissed her forehead in answer. Then he turned to Estie's sister and her fiancé. "Florence, it's a pleasure. Estie told me how you helped her help me find her. Thank you." He inclined his head respectfully. "And Miles, it's good to see you, too."

Miles grinned. "You remembered my name. I'm impressed." He stood and extended a hand. "Welcome to the family, man."

Florence tutted. "Only blood relatives get to say that, babe." She rose, turning to face James. "Welcome to the family, James."

He smiled. "Thanks."

"And call me 'Flo.' Only my mother calls me by my full name."

A familiar voice behind them startled James. "Are you talking about me?"

He turned to find Estie's mother and father, as well as Estie's younger brother and his boyfriend, standing at the patio's entrance. James gave them his best, friendliest smile, despite the slightly queasy sensation in his stomach. Estie must have sensed or anticipated his nerves, because she tightened her grip on his arm, leaning into him in a silent show of support.

"Actually, we were talking about Estie's latest drama." Florence grinned.

Estie's mother clapped her hands together and approached James. "James! We were watching the livestream!" She smiled. "Thank you."

James cleared his throat. "For what, Mrs. Williams?"

"For never giving up on my daughter. For finding her, and not a moment too soon."

Estie's father shook James' hand. "We're glad the two of you are reunited, James. Estie's missed you."

Freddy snorted. "Can't have missed him that much, if she found the time to write a bestseller."

Estie glared at her brother, and opened her mouth to retort, no doubt. Mr. Williams stepped in. "Why don't we all sit down?"

Huffing, Estie allowed James to pull out a chair for her. "Yes, let's order some appetizers. Frederick's always more of a prick when he's hungry."

Her younger brother swooped in for a hug, surprising everyone. Then he turned to James. "In all sincerity, I'm glad you two are back together, dude. Don't ever let that happen again."

James met Estie's eyes as he replied. "I have no intention of letting her out of my sight, ever again."

Estie laughed. "Overkill, James."

He shrugged. "What can I say? I'm a black and white thinker, baby."

"Oh!" Estie's mother beamed. "And he knows his DBT!"

FOREVER AND EVER

"James?" Estie called, closing the door to their apartment on the far side of Blue Sky. "Where are you?"

She placed the groceries on the kitchen counter, shrugged out of her light jacket, then crossed over into the separate living room. "Ja-ames!"

A strum of guitar strings sounded, from the direction of the bedroom. Intrigued, Estie followed the sound. Entering their bedroom, she found blue cornflowers scattered across the coverlet that stretched over their bed. To its left, the sliding glass doors were wide open, leading out to the balcony, which was lit with candles. In the distance, Estie could see Lonely Peak, its craggy lines softened by moonlight.

The love of her life sat out on the balcony, in one of the two chairs they'd built by hand on a whim, strumming his guitar. His hair was as long as it had been when she first met him, and his eyes were as bright and brilliant a green. But what Estie loved best was his smile—no longer so rare, but still every bit as special.

"What's this?" Estie asked as she joined him.

"Take a seat," he said, smiling up at her.

Estie, for once, did as she was told. James began to play in earnest, and Estie recognized the first few notes of "Forever and Ever, Amen." The first song he'd ever sung to her. But not the last. The past six years had been filled with the sound of their laughter and their love-making, her chatter and his singing. Estie closed her eyes and leaned back in her chair and let the sweetest sound in the world wash over her in waves. Forever and ever, indeed.

ACKNOWLEDGMENTS

Almost a year prior to the publication of this novella, my family whisked me away to Montana for a ski holiday. For that, I thank them —although, at the time, I was rather less pleased. I, like Estie, am a terrible skier and would not have left my apartment, much less ventured out onto the slopes of a mountain in the middle of nowhere, without the encouragement of my parents, my siblings, and my siblings-in-law. But had I not gone on that trip, I would never have been inspired to write this.

Writing is about more than inspiration, however. It's hard work, wrangling words, and no one should do it alone. I'd like to thank my editor, Jen, for the structural and emotional support. She's seen me through several manuscripts now and her insights remain invaluable. Thanks, as well, to Grace, my first reader and eventual copyeditor, who texted me mid-read-through to complain that the sex-in-the-snowbank scene was unrealistic as it would have been very cold on that mountainside. I know. And yet…

Lastly, I wish to acknowledge the kindness shown to me by two ski instructors, Gordon and (a different) Grace, as well as their technical ability. Thank you both: for teaching me to ski, for answering my questions, for slowing down the lifts for me—for everything.

ABOUT THE AUTHOR

Phebe Powers cut her teeth on lithium carbonate tablets and historical romance novels. An avid romance reader as well as a firm believer in Happily Ever Afters, she's happiest when tucked away in the basement stacks of her local library, writing her own book or reading someone else's. This is Phebe's first novella.

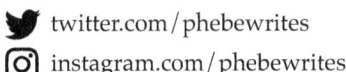

twitter.com/phebewrites

instagram.com/phebewrites